RENEGADES

The Judas War

MICHAEL KOOGLER
SKY CONWAY

Renegades:
The Judas War

By Michael Koogler & Sky Conway

ISBN: 978-1-943519-04-0

Book editing by
Barbara Malmberg, Cedar Rapids, Iowa USA

Book cover art, packaging and design by
Kreative Storm Press, Coralville, Iowa USA

Book Published under AtomicBrain Media,
Malibu, California, USA

*To the wonderful Kickstarter Donors
that helped bring Renegades to life!*

This one's for you!

Acknowledgements From The Authors

Before we get started, we would like to take a moment and acknowledge some key people who have played a big part in making this journey come to life.

First and foremost, I want to thank Sky Conway for giving me the opportunity to become a Renegade and be a part of this incredible experience. Thanks also those members of the crew, including Ryan Husk, Zina Kresin, and Ethan H. Calk, who endured all my emails and questions as I worked to make sure I got everything about this story…right.

Also, a heartfelt thanks goes to Adrienne Wilkinson, who gave me a great lead character in Lexxa. I can't tell you how many times I watched her scenes in the original Renegades pilot episode, in order to capture the spirit of Lexxa. And working on the *Renegades: The Requiem* set with her was truly inspirational.

And finally, a special thanks to my beta-readers, including Zina, as well as my good friend and fellow book geek, Scott Kaalberg and one of my most favorite people/writers in the world, Rachel Aukes. You are all awesome!

~ Michael Koogler

I would like to acknowledge Gene Roddenberry, my inspiration and mentor, Jack Trevino & Ethan H. Calk, wonderful collaborators and true gentlemen. Also, Walter Koenig, my dearest friend, and Nichelle Nichols, my L.A. mom, partner, and the embodiment of Star Trek Ideals.

Tim Russ…you are the Man!

I would also like to express my gratitude for all the actors from *Star Trek: Of Gods and Men*, *Star Trek Renegades*, and *Renegades: The Requiem*. A special thanks goes to our incredible Star Trek alums across the spectrum from *Star Trek: Enterprise* to *Voyager* and every series and movie in between: Walter Koenig, Nichelle Nichols, Alan Ruck, Tim Russ, Gary Graham, Chase Masterson, Garrett Wang, J. G. Hertzler, Crystal Allen, Ethan Phillips, Cirroc Lofton, Lawrence Montaigne, Grace Lee Whitney, Arlene Martel, Manu Intiraymi, Robert Picardo, Courtney Peldon, Clint Carmichael, Richard Herd, Terry Farrell, Robert Beltran, Aron Eisenberg, Hana Hatae, and all of the other amazing actors who have joined me on this journey. None of this would be possible without you.

I also want to express a great big thanks to my incredible crew: Frank Zanca, Tom Moore, Ryan Husk, Linda Zaruches, Scott Nakada, and the hundreds of creative and incredibly talented souls who worked on Renegades.

And finally…Jimmy Doohan, Leonard Nimoy, DeForest Kelly, and Neil Armstrong, I miss your incredible spirits.

~ Sky Conway

Prologue

Sector 6

Earth

With movements that could almost be considered affectionate, slender fingers traced the contours of the young woman's face, feeling the life force that pulsed strongly within her, stronger than any other human. The woman lay peacefully sleeping, unaware of the events surrounding her, as Kovok concentrated, working his thoughts into her neural implant as only he was able.

As he worked, the dark-skinned Sector 6 commander fought to keep his own emotions in check, knowing all too well how much the young woman had suffered already because of the machinations of the Confederation. He still wasn't convinced that what he was doing was right. Necessary, yes. But right?

His fingers worked delicately underneath her eyes and across her temples as he felt the powerful emotions within her mind. The natural telepathic ability he possessed was a gift—a curse maybe?—scientifically augmented by his own position within the black ops arm of the Confederation. He felt as she felt. Knew what she knew. So strong, she was. But so much raw emotion—rage, pain, suffering, despair. He wondered what she could have left within her to keep her going.

And there it was, floating like a beacon of light in her subconscious. He knew what it was even before he touched those thoughts. Her mother. Lexxa lived for her mother. And he immediately understood why. The Confederation, particularly Sector 6, had used her mother. They had used her to birth Lexxa and then had used Lexxa. In doing so, they had sought the perfect weapon, an individual who would be subservient to the powers that be, obeying their every edict.

But those people were gone now, purged from Sector 6 in an internal upheaval that caused the shedding of blood, some of it innocent. But in that uprising, the young Lexxa had been freed from the yoke others would have placed upon her. With Kovok's help, she had escaped the confines of the secret base that had housed her for several years; a place where she had been undergoing conditioning as the former Sector 6 leaders sought to prepare her for deployment into the field.

And now here she was again, back at the same lab where she had been held captive and Kovok was getting ready to use her all over again. Logically, he knew it was for the best; for the very survival of a Confederation he knew was drawing closer to collapse. But the question remained. Was it right?

As he completed his probing of her subconscious and finally drew his hands away from her face, he was aware of one of the scientists standing behind him.

"She is a remarkable specimen," the white-coated man said in wonder, looking down at her peaceful face.

"She is no specimen," Kovok said, his voice cold, almost daring the man to push. "She is a human being."

"Understood sir," the scientist said carefully, lowering his head and backing away. "I meant no disrespect."

Kovok ignored him and looked down at Lexxa's face again. If only he could provide her with a better future. But he could not. This was the only way he knew of ensuring her survival. Of the survival of everyone. And there was no going back, even if it meant using her almost as callously and completely as her handlers had in the past.

As the scientist exited the room, another man entered. He wore a Confederation uniform and insignia, a ranking member of the council and a man that Kovok had known and trusted for years. "You are finished?" the newcomer asked tonelessly, not bothering to look at him.

"It is done, Admiral," Kovok answered. "It will take some time for her to acclimate to what we are expecting her to do, but I foresee no difficulties in accomplishing it."

"Very good," Admiral Armstrong said, looking down at her sleeping features. Tall and imposing with short-cropped hair and a graying beard, Armstrong cut an imposing presence. With a thoughtful look in his eyes, he reached out and touched her cheek with the back of his fingers. "You have done well, Kovok," he went on. "Prepare your final report. We will begin her re-indoctrination tomorrow."

"My suggestion would be to give her more time, sir," Kovok cautioned. "She has lived a hard life."

"I will take your advice under consideration," Armstrong replied in an almost bored tone. "Will there be anything else?"

"If we do this," Kovok said thoughtfully, "and it goes wrong, we risk the destruction of the entire Confederation."

"If we don't, we *guarantee* the destruction of the entire Confederation," he replied, a touch of irritation in his voice. "We have been over this already, Kovok. We have fought for the same thing for years and today, Lexxa must step into her role to do what she was created to do." When he looked up, his gaze left no question that there was to be no more discussion and he was dismissed. Kovok offered him a quick nod, then turned and left.

After a few moments to ensure Kovok would not return, the door in the back of the lab opened up and another man stepped in. He was human, with Asian features, and his eyes gleamed with anticipation. "She is ready then?" he asked pointedly.

"Indeed she is, Masaru," Armstrong replied, reaching up and absently fingering the Confederation insignia on his chest. "Even Kovok could not find it."

"And you are certain the implant will be viable for as many years as it takes to be ready to strike?"

"As long as it takes," Armstrong answered, offering a thin smile, but nothing more. He reached out and touched her cheek again and then let his fingers trace over her raven hair, fanned out on the table around her head. "When it's time for us to move, Lexxa will become the perfect assassin and usher in the destruction of the Confederation as we know it today."

"Excellent," Masaru said. "I will inform the directorate that all is in place."

With that, the two men turned and exited the lab. On the table, the muscle below Lexxa's left eye twitched once. Deep in her mind, Lexxa began to dream.

Chapter I

Delta Omega Battle Group
Risahna Sector, Confederation Space

"Helm, bring us around, heading two two one, mark six," Captain Rob Fredericks commanded as his eyes scanned the holographic battle HUD rotating slowly in the air just to his right. He reached up absently to adjust his glasses, forgetting he hadn't worn them in years. Getting his eyesight perfected had been one of the first things he had done upon entering FleetCom's academy program. But that was a long time ago and he hadn't yet broken himself of the habit of feeling like he had to adjust them. Shaking his head irritably he added, "Kirill, I want full telemetry on the fleet movements and how well the others react to our course change."

"Affirmative, sir," Kirill Goncharov replied crisply, his own eyes focused on his tactical combat display. The Ukrainian-born officer scratched at his short beard, then adjusted his read-out accordingly.

Fredericks shifted his gaze to the bridge's main viewing screen as the huge next generation Confederation battleship, the *Dominant*, crisply executed her maneuver, banking sharply in space. Beyond the *Dominant*, six other Confederation vessels were moving as well, preparing to execute a rescue operation on a damaged Confederation freighter. He caught sight of the *Icarus*, the fleet's newest destroyer, moving in synch with the *Dominant*. He marveled at her sleek lines, knowing better than anyone the firepower the smaller ship was packing. Still, it was nothing compared to what his own ship could do.

The *Icarus* and the *Dominant* were the Confederation's most recent additions. The *Icarus*, under the command of his friend, Captain David Woolston, broke space dock only two months ago, just four weeks after the massive Avenger-class battleship that bore the *Dominant's* name was launched. Both vessels were among the most heavily armed and deadly ships in the fleet, built for a singular purpose – war. For the peaceful life and existence that the Confederation liked to portray, the galaxy was never truly at peace. Flare-ups with enemies, both old and new, continually necessitated the need for greater firepower. And of course, there were always the Umbral. Or worse. Fredericks was a peaceful man, but practical. He understood perfectly that sometimes, it was better to have the bigger gun.

"All support vessels preformed adequately, Captain," Goncharov spoke up, garnering a nod of approval from Fredericks. "The *Arizona* and *Khygan* are now moving to point station. Boards are green."

"Excellent," Fredericks replied, casting a quick look at the HUD and noting that all his ships were in position. "Ninety seconds until simulation start. Inform the fleet, Kirill. I think we're about as ready as we can be for this."

"You think FleetCom will keep us out here?" Goncharov asked, after transmitting the coded 'ready' message. "I mean, if the simulation doesn't come off perfectly this time, how much longer do you think they'll make us drill?"

"Relax, Kirill," Fredericks said with a knowing smile. "You'll be back on earth in plenty of time to take Bernadette out for your anniversary. We aren't due for a long deployment for at least another three months."

"That makes me feel a little better," Goncharov said almost dreamily. "We've been married seven years now."

"Seven good years," Fredericks agreed with a nod. "But if you don't keep your head in the game, it'll be your fault if you don't get back to earth on time and I'm not going to let Bernadette pin that on me."

The first officer cleared his throat and straightened in his seat, feigning embarrassment. "Yes, sir."

Behind him, Fredericks couldn't help but smile. "Give the order, Kirill. Let's see how well we do this time."

Goncharov counted it down. "Attack simulation Delta Three Tango preparing to execute in five, four, three, two, one."

At the word 'one', the screen lit up as an even dozen Rigellian attack cruisers began to appear in space around them, their cloaking devices powering down and their weapons charged. The Rigellians had a wide array of warships, but the fast attack cruisers—known as Ravens due to their onyx coloring and swept back wings, were the oldest and most familiar to the Confederation. In the early days of the first Rigellian War over one hundred years ago, the Ravens had inflicted heavy damage on Confederation ships before their own technology had caught up. Today, the Rigellian attack cruiser was sleeker, much faster, and far deadlier, and a dozen of the smaller ships under the right command could be a formidable match, even for the *Dominant's* battle group.

"And here we go," Fredericks said softly as he watched the battle HUD light up.

"*Icarus* is breaking formation," Goncharov reported. "She's beginning her strafing run."

"Bring us to point, helm," Fredericks said calmly. "Full phasic torpedo spread, attack pattern Beta three."

"Aye, sir," came the reply from the gold-shirted lieutenant operating the massive vessel's helm.

On screen, the torpedo barrage launched and spread out against the Rigellian vessels. Two of the cruisers took moderate hits, while the rest scattered, which was the whole intent. On screen, he watched as the two Confederation destroyers—the *Arizona* and *Khygan*—swept smoothly down below the *Dominant's* bow in pursuit of three of the enemy vessels. On screen, their pulse cannons lit up, cutting across the rear shields of all three vessels. One suffered a catastrophic shield failure and in moments, it was nothing more than an expanding ball of plasma.

"Captain," Science Officer Rydan spoke up quickly. Sykian Rydan was a Krayht, a race similar to humans in behavior and most physical traits, save for their extremely long lifespans. Only two centuries old, Rydan was young for his kind and enjoying his new calling in FleetCom. "Captain Eappen reports that the *Nightingale* is under attack," he said.

"Helm, bring us around," Fredericks answered the unexpected enemy move. If he was upset at the Rigellian's desire to attack a Confederation hospital ship, he didn't show it. He added just as calmly, "Lock pulse cannons." Looking at his tactical hub, he noted the Rigellian had made a direct course change to intercept Eappen's cruiser almost immediately after the attack had begun. Near the *Nightingale* was the *Jonathan Spencer*, a Confederation science cruiser. That vessel was much better armed than the hospital ship, but a well-commanded attack cruiser could be deadly to both of them.

"She's firing torpedoes!" Rydan announced.

"Damn," Fredericks muttered to himself, his fingers quickly tapping the holographic display, keying out an emergency attack pattern in response to the clearly unexpected move. The *Dominant's* pulse cannons answered, the powerful beams cutting through the shields and starboard engine of the enemy cruiser, sending it spinning out of control. "Target that torpedo," he commanded, his voice a bit louder now.

"Weapons locked!"

Before he could give the order to vaporize the torpedo, another vessel shot through his tactical, passing just over the *Dominant's* bridge, her own pulse lances punching through space. The torpedo disappeared in a flare of energy, sparing the *Nightingale* what could have been serious damage.

"Looked like you needed a hand," Captain Woolston's voice rang out smugly over the comm link as the *Icarus* banked again and finished off the wounded Rigellian, before diving back toward another target.

Fredericks ground his teeth together, but didn't give his friend the dignity of a reply. Instead, he issued fleet-wide orders to compensate for the unexpected change in the Rigellian's attack. "*Khygan* and *Arizona*, break off your current attack run and rendezvous with the *Nightingale*. I don't want any other surprise runs against her. Our mission is to break the enemy line, but it won't do us much good if our rescue ship isn't around to take on survivors." After two affirming replies, he went on, addressing the other large battleship within the battle group. "*Nottingham*, what's your status?"

"Two Rigellians are down," came Captain Sullivan's crisp reply. The man was infinitely proud of his ship and his crew and rightfully so. The *Nottingham*—a sovereign-class battleship—had a long and storied career as a Confederation ship-of-the-line. She had completed two deep space exploration missions, as well as been involved in some of FleetCom's more epic battles with a variety of enemies. And through her nearly twenty years in service, Tom Sullivan had been her captain the entire time. "We are in pursuit of a third," he added.

Fredericks didn't need to ask about any damage. His HUD display showed that the *Nottingham* had taken several direct torpedo hits, but had emerged with only moderate damage and no casualties.

"*Icarus* moving to assist the *Nottingham*," Woolston's voice sounded again, apparently taking great pleasure in what the smaller destroyer had been able to do to this point. He wouldn't be lying. The battle HUD told the story. Four of the attackers had been destroyed outright by the *Icarus*. Two more had been rendered immobile. The destroyer was showing that she was everything that FleetCom had hoped she would be. But that didn't mean she could shoulder the entire battle, nor should Woolston try.

"Negative," Fredericks said coolly. "Sullivan has things well in hand, Captain. Bring the *Icarus* back into formation. The enemy is beaten and is retreating. We need to begin the rescue phase."

When there was no reply, Fredericks frowned, his eyes going back to the battle HUD. Rydan's voice confirmed what he saw. "*Icarus* maintaining course, sir. She'll be in range of the *Nottingham* in two minutes."

Fredericks activated his comm. "*Icarus* only," he said curtly, instructing the computer to take him off fleet-wide. Without waiting for the acknowledging beep, he went on. "You might have the prettiest gown at the ball, Woolston, but you are disobeying a direct order. Bring the *Icarus* back in formation."

He was answered only with silence.

"*Captain* Woolston?"

"Sir," Rydan said slowly, eyes on his board. "The *Icarus* has activated her cloak."

"Repeat that?" Fredericks said in near disbelief.

"She's gone to full stealth mode," Rydan confirmed.

"What the hell is Woolston trying to do?" Fredericks was angry now and not bothering to hide it. He'd known Woolston for a number of years and although the brash captain could be a hotshot and headstrong at times, Fredericks couldn't even begin to think what the man was up to. This was supposed to be a routine wargames exercise, nothing more. And using the *Icarus'* cloak was not part of the game. "Kill the simulation, Commander Goncharov," he instructed. "Inform all ships to regroup immediately."

"Yes, sir," Goncharov sighed unhappily, knowing that they were facing another run at the simulation, further delaying his homecoming.

As his first officer went about shutting down the wargame simulation and recalling the fleet, Fredericks scanned his display, waiting for the *Icarus* to reappear and Woolston to laugh about the ploy. Friend or not, though, Fredericks would have some harsh words for the man during the debriefing. On the display, he watched the

Confederation vessels coming about and heading back to the rendezvous point as ordered. All except the *Icarus*. It remained off the grid and the longer he watched and waited for it, the larger the cold pit forming in his gut became.

Finally, he knew enough. "Kirill," he said quickly. "Go to red alert."

"Sir?"

"Do it. Now."

The familiar klaxon began and Captain Fredericks settled into his chair, eyes going to his display. "Fleet wide," he ordered the comm and as it chirped its compliance, he addressed his other captains. "Attention all ships," he said formally. "All ships, red alert. Prepare for battle. This is not a drill."

Chapter 2

Delta Omega Battle Group
Risahna Sector, Confederation Space

"Status report," Captain Woolston of the *Icarus* said quietly as he watched the battle display overlaid on the forward view screen.

"Thirty seconds to target," Lexxa replied, her fingers flying over her control station as she managed the very real part of the wargames exercise, something only Woolston, herself, and a handful of insurgents knew about. "Weapons locked on target. Low yield warheads should take them out of the fight."

"Belay that order, Commander," Woolston countered coldly. "Go to full power on all weapons."

"Sir?" Lexxa questioned, turning and looking at her captain in shock. This wasn't part of the deal and she was not about to lay into a practically defenseless friendly target with full weapons.

"You heard me."

"Captain, we were told to disable only. At that yield, the *Nottingham* won't stand a chance," Lexxa dared to point out. "She's not running with shields."

"I have my orders, Commander," Woolston said dispassionately. "And you have yours. Carry them out."

Lexxa hesitated, considering what to say, but Woolston's glare was enough to turn her back to her board. David Woolston had been her captain since she had reluctantly joined—more like forced to join—

FleetCom on the insistence of a certain Sector 6 commander, some three years prior. Serving first as Woolston's helm officer aboard the *Cherokee*, a Confederation attack frigate, he had brought her over to the *Icarus* with him when he was reassigned to the next gen destroyer, He had immediately appointed her his First Officer and assigned her to tactical, something not uncommon on the smaller destroyers. Her skills at the helm of a warship were superior to most, part of her genetic heritage, she supposed, and something she wasn't at all proud of. But Woolston always said he knew the value of a good officer and so he had put those skills to good use during her time serving under him. In a number of exercises leading up to today, she had shown her ability to pilot the agile destroyer in battle and do it exceptionally well. Today's wargames exercise had proven that even more. And now here she was, getting ready to take out a Confederation sovereign-class battleship on the orders of her captain, who had only recently told her that a schism had developed within the Confederation and he had been ordered to go active during the exercise. He hadn't mentioned anything about targeting a friendly starship for destruction, though.

But Lexxa was a soldier first, so despite serious misgivings about Woolston going off script, she reluctantly obeyed the order. She quickly increased the weapon's power to maximum, adjusting her targeting board. She didn't have to guess as to what would happen to the *Nottingham*. A full-power phasic torpedo spread against an unshielded ship—even a battleship—would cause widespread hull breaches throughout the vessel and buckle the superstructure. The pulse cannons, targeting the cruiser's engineering and bridge would do the rest.

The *Nottingham* had no chance.

"Ten seconds," she said tonelessly, still inwardly wrestling with what she was about to do.

"Lieutenant Jirin," Woolston said, motioning to the officer manning the *Icarus'* science station. "Execute the *Dominant's* restart program."

Jirin nodded and activated the specific program from his board. "Done," was all that he said, looking every bit as grim as Lexxa.

"Drop cloak and prepare to fire," Woolston said with finality.

"Captain Fredericks," Sullivan's voice came over the comm immediately after the red alert message had been broadcast. "What are you talking about? There are no enemy vessels anywhere near us."

"It's the *Icarus*," Frederick's answered quickly. "She's…"

He got no further as the wailing of the klaxon suddenly ceased and power began to cut out to all stations on the bridge. "Status!" he shouted, standing up as his comm crackled and went dead. He knew what was happening already, but no one should have been able to make it happen but himself.

"Full system shut-down, Captain!" Goncharov replied, as his command board flashed red and then went dark. "Sir, I can't stop it!"

"Engineering! What's going on?"

"Captain!" Rydan exclaimed, pointing toward the view screen. "Look!"

All eyes went to the flickering view screen. Before it faded to darkness, each one of them watched as the *Icarus* uncloaked and at nearly point-blank range, unloaded everything she had into the *Nottingham*. Phasic torpedoes ripped through the ship's shields before the destroyer's phased pulse lances punched through the hull, tearing away great portions of the ship. Moments later, the view screen flared with the battleship's destruction and then everything went dark.

"Report!" Fredericks snapped, still trying to piece together what they had just witnessed. A Confederation battle cruiser destroyed. Nearly 700 souls slaughtered. And for what?

"Captain," Rydan pointed out calmly. "All systems are down. We're completely blind."

"Captain Fredericks," Engineer Todd Desiato's voice sounded over the comm system, crackling and faint under emergency power. "We have a total reactor shutdown."

"How?" Fredericks snapped, again more interested in how anyone else could have accomplished the complete power shutdown of his ship. He knew what was supposed to happen during this exercise and had agreed to play is part for the good of the Confederation. But nowhere in his orders was he ever made aware that people would die. Everything had gone completely off script and he was powerless to do anything about it.

"Unknown sir," came the reply. "All systems are down. Auxiliary is down, too, but we should have it up in less than five minutes. We're on emergency battery only at the moment."

"I need full power immediately!" Fredericks snapped, wondering if the *Icarus* was closing on them even now.

"Out of the question, Captain. We'll need a full thirty minutes before we can even think about bringing the mains back online for a cold start."

"We have two minutes."

"Sir," Desiato said helplessly.

"Do it faster!"

A sigh on the other end. Not much had changed for Chief Engineers, dating all the way back to earth's nautical days. "Yes, sir."

"Rydan, get me tactical as soon as you have power," Fredericks said. "I need to see what's happening out there."

"Yes, sir."

Fredericks looked at the screen and shook his head. "What have you done, Woolston?" he said softly.

Captain David Woolston watched the destruction of the *Nottingham* with eyes that were chips of ice. He'd never liked Captain Sullivan, so taking him out along with his ship was a bonus. His orders had been to destroy one of the fleet ships, preferably one of the destroyers. But Woolston felt taking out a battleship was a better test of his ship's power and would generate more shock and outrage in the long run. The *Nottingham* had been the perfect target. Even better would have been eliminating the *Dominant*. But he was under strict orders to not leave her too badly damaged—the operative word being damaged. His superiors had long-term plans for the battleship.

Jirin spoke up from his station. "Captain, the *Khygan* has disabled the *Arizona* as ordered. Captain Gil is reporting the *Nightingale* is retreating with the *Jonathan Spencer* protecting her."

Woolston opened his comm. "Nice work, Captain Gil," he said.

"Let the *Nightingale* go; she's of no consequence."

"Affirmative, sir," Captain Kevin Gil replied back. "We are moving to your position."

"Negative, Captain. Finish off the *Arizona* and then leave the system."

"She's a dead stick, Captain," Gil replied hesitantly. "Engines are down and power is minimal. She's not going anywhere."

"Finish her," Woolston enunciated coldly. "Then proceed to the rendezvous point as ordered."

There was a pause, before the young destroyer captain answered. "Consider it done, sir. Gil out."

Woolston shifted the view screen to show the *Khygan* bank around and make a final run against her sister ship. The *Khygan's* pulse cannons lanced out, cutting through the bridge section of the *Arizona*. Explosions began to hopscotch across the hull before a final torpedo barrage ended her existence, leaving her nothing more than an expanding ball of plasma and debris. A moment later, the *Khygan* vanished as her FTL drive engaged.

"Our work is almost done here, Commander," Woolston said, bringing the tactical grid back up. "Lock weapons on the *Dominant*. Attack pattern Zeta two."

"Are you going to kill them, too?" Lexxa snapped, failing to keep the anger out of her voice this time. She was still reeling from what they had done to the *Nottingham* and even more disquieting, what was happening to the battle group.

"That would be a waste now, wouldn't it?" Woolston smirked, but then went cold again. "Single attack run only; one pulse blast to their bridge ought to do it.”

“You’re going to kill the bridge crew?”

“My orders are to make sure the command structure is incapacitated, commander,” he said icily. “I remind you that my orders are your orders. Are we clear?”

Lexxa did not answer, turning back to her board, readying her weapons. This whole thing was out of control. When Woolston had brought her aboard the *Icarus* as his first officer, it was because of her unwavering loyalty to him, despite the fact that she still wanted no part of FleetCom and the Confederation. However, in spite of all she had experienced in her young life—things that drove most others away from her—Woolston had been there to help her along when she had enlisted. Ostracized most of her life because of who she was, Woolston helped take some of the sting away. He calmly helped her deal with her demons and mentored her through her training before bringing her aboard the *Cherokee* as a cadet, where she worked her way up the command structure in record time. When he was transferred to the *Icarus*, she went with him as his new first officer. But that promotion came with a price. And Woolston had wasted no time in telling her what it was.

“The Confederation is coming apart,” he had told her several weeks before. “It is corrupt, flawed, and long past time to push the reset button.”

“I don’t understand, sir.”

“There is a movement, Lexxa—a movement to take the Confederation back, to strengthen FleetCom, and once again become what we should be.”

"I'm not much of a fan of the Confederation myself," she had answered, thinking back with bitterness to what her life had been before Kovok had convinced her that the Confederation's FleetCom was her best destination. "But I don't understand what you're implying, sir."

"This assignment," he explained, waving his hand in the air to encompass everything all around them, "the *Icarus*. I've been given this assignment as part of a coup that is getting ready to take place."

"A coup?" she'd asked in shock.

"We are taking back the Confederation," Woolston answered, not hiding anything from her. "The *Icarus* is a big part of the opening salvo. And as my first officer, I need to make certain you can be trusted."

"Look, Captain," she'd argued. "I may be FleetCom's black sheep, but taking the *Icarus* for an insurgency? Why?"

"That will be made clear in time," he answered, offering nothing more. "But I remind you of your duty to FleetCom and the oath you took."

"I'm not sure, but I don't remember the word rebellion being anywhere in that oath," she countered.

"Sometimes, you have to be willing to excise the cancer that exists at the heart of what we hold dear. I'll ask you again; do I have your support?"

She had hesitated, but had eventually agreed. "Yes, sir."

And now, she had presided over the death of hundreds of FleetCom personnel, crew members who had no idea what was going to happen to them. With that guilt weighing down on her, she brought the *Icarus* into its attack run and locked a single forward pulse cannon on the *Dominant's* bridge. "Two minutes to optimal firing range, Captain," she announced emotionlessly.

"Very good, Commander," Woolston answered. "No hurry, but you may fire when ready."

One hundred and twenty seconds passed quickly and swallowing the bile that rose in her throat, she obeyed her captain. The blast took out the forward portion of the *Dominant's* bridge, much less than what Woolston had been expecting, but she moved the *Icarus* away from the wounded ship before he could visually ascertain that she had deliberately dialed back the power on the shot, hoping to spare some of the bridge crew.

"Report," he said coldly as he watched the *Dominant* slide from the view screen, trailing debris.

"Full hull breach," Jirin replied quickly from his station, his eyes darting briefly toward the first officer. He knew what she had done, but he had no idea why. "Their bridge is dead, Captain," he said, covering up Lexxa's disobedience. "They will not be following us."

"Thank you, Jirin," Woolston said. "Set course for the rendezvous point. We have a meeting to attend."

Moments later, the *Icarus* engaged her FTL drive and vanished into deep space.

Chapter 3

Dominant

Risahna Sector, Confederation Space

Sykian Rydan was floating. As he reached up and slowly wiped the blood from his eyes, he realized he wasn't the only one. There were bodies in the air around him. The top of the bridge had been ripped open and the only thing keeping him and the rest of the bridge crew from being sucked into the cold vacuum of space was the emergency force field that he could see faintly shimmering above him. That sparked a rather disquieting thought. On battery power, he wasn't sure how long the force field would last.

Wincing in pain, he turned himself in the zero gravity and tried to take stock of the situation. That he was alive seemed to be a miracle, because judging by what he saw of most of the rest of the bridge personnel, he wasn't sure anyone else had survived.

Opening his personal comm, he managed to croak, "Engineering. Status report."

"What happened, commander?" came Desiato's quick reply. It was obvious the man did not yet know what had just occurred.

"Uncertain…at the moment," Rydan said, catching hold of the command chair and righting himself. Reaching out a hand, he grasped Captain Fredericks' sleeve and slowly rotated him in the air. The man's eyes were open and fixed. The scorched hole in his chest confirmed his fear. "Captain Fredericks is dead," he added quietly.

"Dead?"

"Lieutenant Desiato, can you restore gravity to the bridge?" Rydan asked, feeling no need to confirm the death announcement.

"Aye, sir," the chief engineer replied. "It'll take a minute, but I'll have it back up shortly. I can't promise I can keep it active, though, until we begin restoring full power."

"Understood," the Krayht replied, "but only on my command. Everyone here is floating in zero G. If anyone else is alive, I don't want them crashing back to the deck when the gravity comes back."

"Yes, sir. Commander, what happened?" Desiato asked again.

"We appear to have suffered a weapon's hit, likely phased pulse fire from one of our own," Rydan replied, looking around. Besides the tear in the hull above him, the rest of the bridge looked relatively unscathed. If it was indeed a pulse hit, it wasn't full power or there would be nothing left and he wouldn't be floating here wondering what had happened. "The bridge has been compromised," he went on. "The protective force field is in place, but we'll need space dock for repairs."

"What about everyone else?"

"Unknown at the moment," Rydan answered, not wanting to give voice to what he already felt was true. "Get me a Medical team to the bridge and make sure they have gravity boots."

"Done, sir."

Rydan tapped the link closed and began moving carefully about the bridge, checking on his crewmates. When he was done, only one of the eleven was still alive. Lieutenant Carly Creer, better known to her crewmates as Shibby, the *Dominant's* communications officer, was unconscious and had a nasty gash on the back of her head. Beyond that, she appeared to be not too badly hurt. The rest had been killed, including the captain and First Officer Kirill Goncharov. That left him the senior officer onboard. The *Dominant* was now his. It was definitely not the way he ever anticipated getting a command and he wasn't certain he even wanted one. But regardless, he knew it would be a short one; just long enough to get the battleship back to earth space dock where FleetCom would assign the *Dominant* a new captain and bridge crew.

The Medical team arrived, coming up through a crawl tube, as the lifts were inoperative. He had already pulled Lieutenant Creer to the floor, so she wasn't further injured by falling when gravity was restored.

"How many casualties?" Doctor Camden asked, looking harried. The young surgeon had a knack for appearing older than he really was. But he was one of the best and only the best had been assigned to the *Dominant.*

"Except for Lieutenant Creer," Rydan said sadly, "all of them."

Doc shook his head angrily and moved toward the prone communications officer. "Someone better tell me how this happened when we were supposed to be in a training exercise."

"When I have all the answers, I'll be sure to inform you, doctor," Rydan said. He again signaled Desiato. "Lieutenant, you can restore gravity."

There was a slight hum through the bridge and suddenly, ten bodies were dropping to the floor. Rydan winced at the sound, but he didn't have a choice. The Medical team could take care of the dead. He had work to do.

"How soon can you get me auxiliary?" he asked Desiato as he watched the med team get to work.

"Spooling up the generators now, sir," came the reply.

"And FTL capabilities?"

"Thirty minutes before I can begin a cold start. Whatever happened triggered a complete shutdown of all our systems and it blew out our redundant backups."

"In other words, what wasn't supposed to ever happen, did."

"That's the way it looks, sir," Desiato replied. "Pretty clear that it's sabotage, sir," he added, giving voice to Rydan's thoughts.

Only Rydan had already taken it to the next level and was wondering how Captain Woolston of the *Icarus* had pulled it off. He could think of no other culprit. "It looks that way," he said thoughtfully. "Do we have subspace communications?"

"Yes, sir. No damage to the communications systems."

Nodding, Rydan walked to the ready room, leaving the Medical team to their duties. Once there, he hesitated before taking a seat in what used to be the captain's chair. To say he was uncomfortable was not telling the half of it. After a few moments, he activated the console with his command override code, requested a priority one scrambled channel, and then keyed in the admiral.

Admiral Dianne Doyle came on screen less than a minute later. "Captain Fredericks," she began lightly, before seeing that it was not the captain of the *Dominant* on the other end at all. "Commander Rydan," she corrected herself, her brows furrowing at the unexpected sight of the Krayht contacting her on the captain's secured channel. Her instincts, however, did not miss that something was dreadfully wrong. She was immediately all business. "Report," she snapped.

"We have been attacked," Rydan answered evenly, keeping his composure. "We are still ascertaining the damage."

"Who?"

"Best guess at the moment is that it was Captain Woolston and the *Icarus*. We saw him attack and destroy the *Nottingham*, before something shut down all our power systems. Redundant backups and relays were all disabled. Whoever did it, knew exactly what they were doing."

"What is your current status, Commander?"

"The bridge was hit by what I believe to be a low level phased pulse blast," he answered. "I'm not certain of the reason, but we were without shields at the time and they could have hit us a lot harder. However, the damage to the outer bridge hull is still extensive."

"Casualties?"

"Of the acting bridge personnel, only Lieutenant Creer and I survived," he answered, swallowing the lump in his throat. "Captain Fredericks is dead."

"As is Commander Goncharov?" she surmised.

"Yes, ma'am."

"Then you are acting captain, Sykian Rydan," she said, showing no qualms about tagging him with that title, even though it made him extremely uncomfortable. "I'll make the proper protocol changes on my end."

"Yes, ma'am," he said, forcing his breathing and heartrate to remain even.

"When will you have full power?"

"We can begin a cold start in about thirty minutes," he replied.

"Two hours from now, we should have all systems restored and can return to earth space dock."

"Negative, Captain," she said, her tone clipped. "You will pursue the *Icarus* as soon as you have full power."

"I'm sorry, Admiral?" Rydan questioned.

"I hate to say this, but if what you said about Captain Woolston is true, I can't say I'm terribly surprised."

"You knew this would happen?" Rydan said, feeling his temper suddenly rising.

"If you're asking if I had direct knowledge of this, then not at all," she answered. "But I have long suspected something more has been at work in the Confederation."

"What exactly?"

"It's far too early to lay it all out, Captain, and we have too little time," she answered. "As I said, once you have full capabilities, you are to find the *Icarus*."

"We have a serious hull breach, Admiral," Rydan dared to argue. "We cannot possibly go into battle."

"You'll follow orders, Captain."

"But I have no command crew," Rydan added, feeling completely helpless.

"Then you'll promote one," Doyle said, her voice hard.

Rydan almost added more, but the admiral's eyes told him that would not be a good idea, so he bit back his reply and simply nodded.

"Let me remind you of your duties, Captain," Doyle continued, leaning forward, her gaze hard. But just as quickly, it softened, as she recognized what the new captain must be experiencing at the moment.

"Look, Sykian," she said, her voice softer. "We're all in a precarious situation now. The *Dominant* is a next generation battleship, the best that the Confederation has ever constructed. She's built to handle a lot more than what you have shared with me. You're captain now and as captain, you need to carry out your orders. You will pursue the *Icarus*, apprehend if possible, but destroy if necessary. I have full confidence in you and your ship."

"Yes, ma'am," he answered shakily. "I'll seal the main bridge bulkheads and transfer command to the battle bridge," he added. "We can operate at full efficiency from there. I'll keep you informed once we have regained full power."

"See that you do, Captain," she said. "And Sykian?"

"Yes, ma'am?"

"Good luck."

The screen went blank. Sykian Rydan sighed deeply and sat for several minutes, staring at the darkened screen, his mind working furiously. Eventually, he keyed his comm, his mouth hardening into a thin line of growing resolve as a plan began to form in his mind.

"Lieutenant Desiato," he said.

"Yes, sir," the chief engineer's voice quickly replied.

"As soon as medical completes their duties, I want an engineering team up here to seal the main bridge."

"Sir, if we're going back to space dock, there's no need to…"

"We aren't going back to earth," Rydan interrupted him. "I want the bridge sealed and starship control transferred to the battle bridge."

"Sir?"

"I'll need full sensors and battle capabilities as soon as possible."

"Yes, sir," Desiato said, knowing not to question anymore.

Rydan tapped the comm link closed and quickly pulled up a list of all senior officers. It took fifteen minutes to identify his new command crew. Once he had, he promoted each of them in the ships database and filed his decisions with FleetCom, then instructed to computer to request each of the crew members report to the battle bridge.

Fifteen minutes later, he was staring at seven wide-eyed personnel and telling them it was time to go to work.

Chapter 4

Icarus

Kabala Sector, Confederation Space

Sitting on her heels in the darkness, she focused her eyes on her target while slowly spinning the deadly blade between her slender fingers. A laser pistol would be quicker, a phased hand cannon messier, but the knife would be more personal. And this was personal.

For practically being a legend in FleetCom, her chosen victim didn't appear to be in any hurry, nor did he appear to be all that concerned for his immediate safety. But Lexxa knew better than to underestimate the man. He'd been alive for a long time and much of that was because he was anything but careless. Even in the San Francisco complex where his living suite was located, she knew he was aware of everything around him, processing everything that might be considered a threat. But he couldn't possibly suspect she was on the premises.

The Admiral shook hands with the security officer that had accompanied him and then turned and began walking toward the elevator. Toward her. She watched him sigh wearily and noted that his shoulders seemed to sag as if a great weight had been placed on them. Not that she cared. She'd happily kill the man, knowing he was distressed about something. It just added to the revenge factor.

Twenty steps away and she flipped the blade up against her forearm and straightened. The plan was simple. The Admiral would walk right by her and she'd cut his throat before he even knew she was there.

Ten steps away, he paused, his gait slowing as his eyes took in the shadowed recess where she was hiding. Something in his eyes told her that he suspected someone was there. As his hand reached toward the weapon at his belt, she rushed out, leading with her blade.

Lexxa sat up, screaming her rage, her eyes blinking open in the darkness of her quarters. At her movement, the lights came up slowly, revealing her quarters aboard the *Icarus*. The dream—the nightmare—was still fresh in her mind, as was the anger she felt toward The Admiral and her nearly rabid desire to kill him. It was all there.

But why?

She bowed her head and closed her eyes tightly. Taking a cleansing breath, she finally swung her feet over the side of her bunk. Deep in her mind, someone was screaming at her that The Admiral must die, but with some effort, she brushed it aside and let her subconscious absorb it. There were far too many other pressing matters to deal with than to let the stupid dream get the best of her again.

She knew what it was; what caused the unsettling nightmare to revisit her after she'd gone weeks without having to deal with it. It was the situation they were currently in. The *Icarus*. Captain Woolston. And most importantly, her hand in the destruction of the *Nottingham*. All those people, dead because of her. And for what?

Anger seeped back into her, but this time it wasn't the unexplained anger that seemed to be growing toward an admiral she barely knew. It was fury at her captain and his orders that forced her to destroy the battleship. It was frustration at knowing enough to know they were trying to right the Confederation and to root out a deep-seated corruption, but not enough to understand why the deaths of innocents had to drench her hands with blood.

Clenching her jaw, she stood and padded across the room to her wardrobe. She dressed quickly in her command uniform, pausing briefly to run her finger across the three collar studs, showing her new rank as commander—first officer of the *Icarus*. It was almost surreal. She'd never wanted FleetCom, never aspired to anything beyond being free to live her life outside the confines of the Confederation, to one day find her mother. But Kovok and Sector 6 had different plans. They'd always had different plans. And now here she was.

Commander.

It still didn't fit her, and she doubted it ever would. And now, the questions arose within her, worming its way up from the depths. Was the price too high? Had Kovok's insistence that she join FleetCom put her in this position, where she had inadvertently become the executioner? Or had it all been by careful design?

Growling audibly, she bit back her resentment and straightened her tunic. She didn't bother checking the mirror, not that she ever did. Right now, she had a way to channel her anger. She'd killed the crew of the *Nottingham*. But it was not her order or desire to. It was Captain Woolston's. And it was time for some answers.

She exited her quarters and immediately ran into another officer. "Walko," she said, her voice sounding startled.

"Sorry, Lexxa," the man replied softly, grasping her arm to keep them both on their feet. Lieutenant Gregg Walko was part of tactical, a friend of Lexxa's and one of her only ones aboard the *Icarus*. "You okay?" he asked.

"Does it look like I'm okay?" she replied, her voice bitter.

"I just wanted to see how you were handling things," he went on. "I heard about what happened. It's hard to even know what to say about it, but you can't blame yourself. You had to follow orders."

"Did I?" she snapped.

"You know the answer to that as well as anyone," he said, his voice still calm. "Something is going on and Captain Woolston seems to know what it is. I just…"

"Look, Walko. Just be glad you weren't in the chair," she sighed.

"I am," he nodded sadly. "I just wish it weren't at your expense."

"Not much I can do about what has happened," she shrugged and then pushed past him. "But maybe I can do something about what will happen."

"What do you mean?"

"I'm going to confront Woolston."

"Are you sure that's a good idea, Lexxa?" he asked, causing her to pause and face him again.

"Do you have a better idea?" When Walko couldn't respond, she simply nodded. "I have to," was all she said.

"Just be careful," he cautioned.

She nodded again and then turned away, hurrying down the passage toward the rear of the ship and the captain's quarters. The *Icarus* was a destroyer, much smaller than the cruisers of the Confederation. It only took her a minute to reach the captain's door and she immediately buzzed. There was only a short pause before a gruff "Come," sounded from within.

The door slid open and she stepped inside, allowing her eyes to readjust to the gloom. If she had thought Captain Woolston might be taking advantage of the long FTL journey to their destination to catch some sleep, she was disappointed. His bed looked slightly rumpled, but unslept in. Woolston himself was standing, his eyes staring out into space through the floor-to-ceiling viewing window. The wobbly streaks of stars passed by and not for the first time, she wondered how he could stand and stare at them for so long. He seemed to always enjoy them. It always made her nauseous and she much preferred the view of real-time space.

"Captain," she barked out, a little more angrily than she had intended.

Woolston did not turn around immediately, but merely said softly, "Speak your mind, Commander."

"I don't know if that's a good idea, sir," she bristled. "I might say something I'll regret."

This time Captain Woolston did turn around. He was still in his own command uniform, but he held a small glass in his hand. The remains of a blue liquid swirled at the bottom. "Since when have you ever worried about saying something you would regret, Commander?" he chuckled humorlessly, before tossing back the last bit of Rigellian Ale and setting the empty glass on a nearby table, none too gently. There was a decanter of the liquid on the table as well, more than half empty.

"Are you drunk, sir?" Lexxa dared to ask, cocking her head slightly as if she might see him in a different light.

"Not near as much as I'd like to be," he answered. "But I imagine that your presence here means I'm not done drinking yet."

"I didn't come to drink with you, sir."

"And I didn't invite you to," Woolston snapped back, his tone stinging the young officer more than she cared to admit. "Speak your mind, Commander. I have other things I need to attend to."

Lexxa glanced at the bottle of Rigellian Ale, but bit back the reply that was on the tip of her tongue. She was mad enough at Woolston. No need to get him pissed off at her before she could speak her peace. "Sir," she began, "about the attack."

"You're still angry about the *Nottingham*," he guessed. "What's to be angry about, Commander," he went on, like it meant nothing to him. "You notched the first blow in the insurgency, nothing more. I promise you, before all is said and done, no one will remember the *Nottingham*."

"But why, sir?" she pressed, feeling the guilt rising up within her again.

"Because I ordered you to," Woolston replied evenly. "And I can tell that even by following orders, you're still troubled by it."

"I am."

"I have known you since you came up in FleetCom, Lexxa," he reverted to her first name. Whether it was because he was slightly drunk or something else, she wasn't sure. "I also know your penchant for wearing your emotions under a thin veil," he added.

"But I killed those people," she pleaded, seeking absolution in some way, but knowing that nothing he could say would ease the feelings of remorse that weighed her down.

"In case you need to be reminded, Commander, we are at war.

This insurgency is about the survival of the Confederation and in its execution, there will be casualties. Many casualties."

"But they were innocent, sir."

"None of us are innocent," he countered.

"Damn it, sir!" she snapped. "Give me something to go on here! I saw the original orders! We were to strike a non-lethal blow and liberate the *Icarus*, putting her under direct control of Sector 6. Non-lethal!" she repeated, nearly shouting now.

"You saw the original orders," Woolston said coldly. "Those orders were amended shortly before the simulation. Blood needed to be spilled."

"But why?" she asked again in exasperation. "What purpose does killing the entire crew of a battleship serve?"

"FleetCom has a new directive, commander," he answered. "And that is to survive."

"At what cost, sir?"

"There's a lot more here at stake than you are privy to, Commander."

"Then enlighten me, sir."

"I share with you what information I deem necessary," he snapped. "And right now, you know exactly what you should know and nothing more. I will, however, remind you that you are my first officer and as my first officer, I expect you to obey my orders without question. Do I make myself understood, Commander?"

Lexxa bit her tongue and straightened her back, pushing her chin out in silent defiance. "Yes, sir," she said quickly, unwilling to go any further. She already knew that she had pushed him further than was wise. There would be future repercussions, of that she was certain.

"You are dismissed, Commander," Woolston said, his voice steely. Turning back to the window, he added, "Now get out."

Lexxa allowed herself a sigh and then without a word, she turned and departed, leaving her captain to continue brooding in the dark. She was plenty angry with him, but despite his coldness and rigidity toward her, she realized something.

Captain Woolston was plenty upset, too. As she made her way to the bridge, she wondered at what.

Chapter 5

Icarus

Kabala Sector, Confederation Space

With Captain Woolston in his command chair, the *Icarus* disengaged her FTL drives at the designated coordinates. At her tactical station, Lexxa read the incoming data and reported. "Two vessels at station, sir," she said, fighting to keep the coldness out of her voice. She was still angry at him and not sure she ever wouldn't be.

"Identification?" he asked, his own voice belaying no indication that he harbored any lingering resentment toward her.

"It's the *Khygan* and an unidentified ship," she answered. "It's Rigellian, a Craven-class battle cruiser, but it isn't broadcasting any transponder or identifier."

"Magnified visual," Woolston ordered. On his command, the view screen zoomed in, showing the two vessels. The Confederation destroyer and the older, but no less imposing, Rigellian battle cruiser both hung in space. "Open a channel."

"Channel open, sir," the comm officer replied.

"Captain Gil, status report?"

"We are still working on repairs sir," Gil's voice came back over the comm as the screen lit up to show his image. Behind him, several techs were working on station boards that were dark and looked damaged. "We took more of a pounding than we anticipated."

"When will you be fully battle ready?"

39

There was a pause, before Gil answered. "Another six hours, and we should have full weapons capabilities."

"Captain Karak," Woolston said. "Is your vessel ready?"

The bridge screen split, showing a heavily scarred Rigellian captain, seated in his command chair. "We are prepared," he growled.

"Are you committed to this endeavor?" Woolston asked. It was not the first time he had addressed Karak this way. The Rigellian commander was truly old-school, which was why Woolston had suggested he be brought into the insurgency. Woolston knew the Rigellian preferred an empire at war and the aging treaty with the Confederation was supremely distasteful to him, along with many others in the Empire. Truth be told, the Rigellian captain would be happiest if he was trading weapon's fire with the *Icarus*, rather than bandying words. But he knew Karak was smart, too, and that allying with the insurgency in this way would bring about exactly what the Rigellian wanted—a Confederation weakened and at war with his people. What Karak didn't know was that Woolston and his superiors viewed the Rigellians much the same way they viewed the other alien races; a cancer on the Confederation and something to be ultimately removed. But that time was not now, so Woolston would use the Rigellian to further fan the flames of the rebellion.

"We are prepared to do our part," Karak practically snarled.

"Excellent, Captain," Woolston replied coolly, refusing to get drawn into a heated exchange with the Rigellian. It would be pointless anyway. Karak's orders were to use the *RDF Venomous* to hit a Confederation colony, with the *Khygan* providing support. It wasn't so much about an act of war, but a demonstration of two alien captains—

Gil and most of the *Khygan's* crew was Cyrolian—conspiring to attack a Confederation outpost populated solely by humans. The proposed slaughter was designed to help galvanize support within the more hardline parts of the Confederation for the insurgency and begin laying the groundwork for the future purging. That the current sitting Confederation president was visiting immediate family members living on the colony was an added bonus. Once the attack was carried out, Woolston's orders were to destroy the *Venomous* and the *Khygan* at the second rendezvous point and then go into hiding. The first rule of assassination was to kill the assassins and he would relish the opportunity to kill the wretched Rigellian and the Cyrolian crew of the *Khygan*. The *Icarus* herself would then be saved for operations closer to the commencement of the planned purge.

"You have the coordinates," Woolston went on, "and your orders. Leave some survivors, if possible, but make certain they know who is attacking them. You'll have approximately eighteen minutes before a Confederation patrol will arrive in system in response to your attack. By that time, the damage will have been done."

"For the Rigellian Empire," Karak snapped, before the visual cut out.

"No, my foolish captain," Woolston said softly under his breath. "For the new Confederation."

"Captain," Lexxa spoke up. "New contact bearing one three six, mark three. Intercept course!"

"Visual," Woolston said quickly.

The screen terminated Gil's feed and switched to a magnified view of a starship bearing down on them. There was little doubt who it was.

"It's the *Dominant*, sir," Lexxa said, her voice sounding slightly uncertain.

"And how, pray tell, have they repaired the damage and gotten here so quickly?" Woolston asked, his tone almost accusatory.

"Unknown, sir," Jirin spoke up from his station, once again coming to the first officer's aid. Jirin did not know exactly what was happening between his Captain and First Officer, but he'd had his suspicions for a while now. And he liked Lexxa. When she had deliberately dialed down the power on the attack run against the *Dominant*, he found he liked her even more. "I monitored the attack, sir," he went on. "The bridge was destroyed."

"Captain, we are being hailed," the comm officer reported.

"Hailed?" Woolston repeated, smirking. "Captain Fredericks isn't requesting we surrender already, is he?"

"No, sir."

"Put him on screen," Woolston shrugged. "Let's see what he has to say."

The screen wavered for a moment and then switched to a view of what was clearly a battle bridge.

"Well that explains how they got to us so quickly," Woolston muttered. But he didn't recognize the man sitting in the captain's chair. "State your purpose, Commander," he said aloud with a hint of anger. "Your presence here is interfering in a top secret FleetCom operation."

"Captain Woolston," the man replied, remaining seated, his countenance firm and unwavering. "I am hereby ordering you…"

"Who are you?" Woolston interrupted, in no mood to deal with an underling. "Where's Captain Fredericks?"

"Captain Fredericks was KIA," came the icy reply. "I am Sykian Rydan and I have been formally named captain of the *Dominant*."

"Is that so?"

"It is."

"Well, welcome to the big leagues, *Captain* Rydan," Woolston sneered, not altogether unhappy that Fredericks had died. The two men had been friends for years, but Fredericks had shown an unwavering refusal to listen to Woolston's dire warnings about the weakening of the Confederation. Woolston had decided months ago that he would eventually need to terminate their friendship in a permanent manner. That Fredericks had been killed was a good thing, because it also meant the *Dominant* was in much less capable hands.

"Captain Woolston," Rydan went on. "Under direct orders from FleetCom, you are hereby ordered to stand down and prepare to be boarded, where you will deliver yourself over to custody."

"On who's orders?"

"Admiral Doyle's," Rydan replied. "You have sixty seconds to comply."

Woolston made a slashing motion across his throat and his communications officer cut the feed. The screen showed the *Dominant* still bearing down on them.

"Sir, the *Venomous* is powering up weapons," Lexxa reported.

"Tell Karak to stand down and depart the system immediately," Woolston advised. "His ship would be no match for the *Dominant*. He needs to stick with the plan. We can deal with the *Dominant* ourselves."

"Sir," the communications officer added, looking up in surprise from her board. "Captain Gil is offering his surrender to the captain of the *Dominant.*"

"What?" Woolston snapped, whirling around to look at her.

"I picked up his communication," she replied. "He reported the *Khygan* was unable to offer resistance and he offered his surrender for concessions to his crew."

Woolston whirled back to the screen, anger beginning to etch his features. "Power weapons. Ahead full. Target the *Khygan.*"

"Sir!" Lexxa snapped, looking at him in shock. "There are over 300 men and women aboard the *Khygan!*"

"You've already killed twice that," Woolston seethed. "Target that ship. Now!"

"Captain, I object to this course of action!"

"Duly noted. Now carry out your orders, Commander."

"Sir…."

"NOW!" he roared, jumping to his feet and lunging toward her.

Lexxa was quicker, rolling out of her chair and shoving his grasping hand away from her shoulder.

"Commander," he snapped furiously as she faced him, his features twisted in anger. "You are hereby relieved of duty and are under arrest."

"And you are unfit for command, Captain," she growled back, keeping her voice low and controlled. "You are not yourself, Captain Woolston. You have to see that this is wrong!"

"Security," Woolston said, his façade suddenly turning icy again. "Detain the Commander and put her to the brig."

Lexxa saw the beefy security guard nod hesitantly before raising his energy weapon and beginning to move toward her. For a brief moment, it looked like Jirin would intervene, but his slight movement ceased and he watched the drama unfold, his face unreadable.

She knew she had no chance. For a second, she considered attacking Woolston, but if she ever thought she would have an opportunity to talk him down from wherever it was he had gone, inflicting bodily injury to him now would not help her cause. "Captain," she said, her voice softer as she raised her hands in surrender. "I implore you to…"

At a nod from Woolston, the security officer shot her in the chest. As she crumpled to the deck, unconscious, Woolston turned his back on her and reseated himself in his chair. "Get her out of here," he ordered. "Put her in the brig and leave her. I'll deal with her later."

"Yes, sir," the big man said as he holstered his sidearm. Reaching down, he effortlessly lifted the young woman up and draped her limp form over his shoulder. Without another word, he turned and left the bridge.

"Lieutenant Akashi," Woolston said, turning to one of his other bridge officers. "Take over on tactical and carry out my orders."

"Yes, sir," the man said without hesitating. He quickly slid into Lexxa's chair and powered up weapons.

"Fire when ready, lieutenant," Woolston said. "But leave something for the *Dominant* to pick up."

"Yes, sir," Akashi replied, targeting the various weapons of the *Icarus* onto specific areas of the *Khygan*.

Despite repeated hails from both the *Dominant* and the *Khygan*, the *Icarus* bore down on the damaged destroyer. A targeted spread of torpedoes, followed by precision phased pulse strikes, made short work of the vessel's weakened shields and tore through her superstructure, damaging or destroying critical systems. As the *Icarus* activated her FTL drives, the *Khygan* began ejecting escape pods.

It had all taken less than thirty seconds.

"Captain," Lieutenant Antony Curtis, the *Dominant's* newly assigned science officer, said somberly. With Lieutenant Creer currently being treated in sick bay, he was also doubling as a comm officer on the cramped battle bridge, still rather shocked at his overall promotion to bridge officer. "Damage to the *Khygan* is critical. All power systems offline. Life support is gone."

"Can we raise them on comms?" Captain Rydan asked calmly.

"Negative sir," Curtis answered. "They are completely without power."

"How many survivors?"

"Twenty-seven on board. Sixty-one in escape pods."

"That leaves a lot of dead men and women," Rydan said softly, knowing that there had originally been more than twice that many onboard the ship. "Bring us in. Alert Medical to prepare for casualties. All transporter rooms, prepare to begin beaming over the wounded."

"Sir," he said, looking over her board. "We aren't prepared to take on this many wounded."

"I agree," Rydan said. "Contact Captain Eappen of the *Nightingale.* He's the closet to us. Tell him to make best possible speed to our location."

"And the *Icarus,* sir?"

"We'll deal with that later," Rydan said. "Right now, we have lives to save."

"Yes, sir."

Sykian Rydan watched his display somberly, lamenting the needless slaughter of more FleetCom personnel. Too many people had died today. Somehow, he had to stop Captain Woolston and the *Icarus*. Rydan had the ship that could do it. Unfortunately, he would have to find them first.

48

Chapter 6

Icarus

Trigani System, Confederation Space

Lexxa watched the light fade from behind The Admiral's eyes as the rush of blood from his slit throat slowed its frenzied pumping. She still held his upper arm, keeping him from slumping to the floor, as she watched his chest struggle for one last ragged breath before his eyes finally rolled back in his head.

The Admiral was dead.

And she had killed him.

She raised the murder weapon, the deadly dagger and brought it up to her face. The man's blood streaked the blade where she had slashed his throat and she marveled for a moment that the red liquid held both life and death within it. With it, life flourished, bright and alive. Without it, life was only so much lifeless organic matter. It struck her as odd that such a thought would rivet her like that.

Finish it.

Lexxa started, her head spinning around to catch the speaker. She had been meticulous, planning The Admiral's murder to make sure no one else would be around. So the thought that someone had found her was borderline irrational. And she was correct.

There was no one there.

Finish it, now!

Her eyes were drawn back to the blade and she looked closer at it, contemplating the bloody edge and the pointed tip of it. Raising it, she focused on the dagger's point, angling it so it was directly in front of her eye. So sharp, so deadly. It wouldn't take much. A slight push and she would be free.

Yes, freedom. This will make you free.

With a final sigh, she nodded slightly and obeying the whispered command, she drove the dagger home.

Lexxa awoke, her dying breath still on her lips.

"Shhh!" a voice hissed in the darkness, hands reaching for her.

Panic overtook her and she nearly screamed before a hand clamped tightly over her mouth, forcibly shushing her. Reality roared back in that moment, even as she grabbed for the dagger, desperate to pull it out of her eye. But there was no dagger. She hadn't driven it into her brain and killed herself. And just like that, the dream began to fade and she felt herself begin to relax. She supposed she should be relieved, but there was still the matter of waking up in her darkened cell with someone holding a rough hand over her mouth.

"Lexxa," the voice hissed again. "It's me. Don't scream."

"Walko?" she whispered as the man slowly pulled his hand away. A moment later, a small light flared to life, illuminating the man's face. "What are you doing here?"

"Look, we don't have much time." His voice was hurried and he looked over his shoulder into the darkened security room.

"Time is all I have, Walko," she replied sourly. "I'll be lucky if Woolston doesn't shove me out of an airlock before we make space dock. And he'll do the same to you if he finds you here."

"You're closer to the truth than you know," Walko nodded. "The captain…Lexxa, he's gone off the deep end."

"You mean any more than he already has?"

"He's planning to take out the *Dominant*."

"He'll lose," she countered. "The *Icarus* might be able to take on most vessels in a fight, but the *Dominant* is a battleship; it's next gen, just like this one. They won't get caught unawares again, either."

"They're lucky you were manning tactical in the first place."

"You know about that?" she asked, narrowing her eyes.

"Woolston pulled all the data from the fight after you went rogue, at least that's what he's calling your actions. He saw you dialed down the power and he wasn't too pleased. I've never heard him lose it like that."

"What's his plan?"

"I don't know, beyond making sure he deals with you before anything else goes down," he answered.

"He said he's going to kill me?" she asked, already knowing that was probably what the captain was planning for her. It wouldn't be like him to leave a loose end untied. And she was definitely a loose end.

Walko nodded slowly. "Not in so many words, but the implication is there. He said he can't afford to let you jeopardize his mission."

"How'd you hear about this?" Lexxa asked, trying to keep the desperation out of her voice. She knew she had stumbled into it badly with Woolston and at the moment, she didn't see any way out.

"The captain called an emergency senior staff meeting and I represent tactical now that you're gone," he said sheepishly.

"But he's a FleetCom captain," she started to object. "How can he get away with this?"

"He has an agenda, Lexxa. And he's got support from most of the senior staff."

"What, to murder me?"

"To see that the job is done without interference," Walko responded. "It doesn't take a genius to figure out that he's referring to you."

"This can't be happening," Lexxa said softly, running a worried hand through her long hair.

"Unfortunately, it is. He has Akashi plotting attack patterns specifically for the *Dominant* and it sounds like he has like-minded people already onboard that ship that are going to help him eliminate the *Dominant* as a threat."

"A mutiny?"

"Afraid so," Walko answered grimly. He stood, reaching down to offer Lexxa a hand up. "But if we're going to save both them and ourselves, we need to get off the *Icarus*."

"You have a plan?" Lexxa dared to ask.

"Nothing beyond knowing we need to steal one of the long-range shuttles and somehow launch and be gone before the *Icarus* can bring weapons to bear."

"Beyond the *Dominant*, there's nothing like this ship in the Confederation," she pointed out, shaking her head. "We won't stand a chance if we don't even the odds."

"How?"

"We'll need to disable main power if we're going to pull this off."

"Look, we don't have a lot of time, Lexxa," Walko warned. "Woolston isn't going to wait around. He is going to kill you. If we don't get off the ship now, we don't get off at all."

Without waiting for a reply, the tactical officer hurried to the room's entry door, letting it slide silently open. He peered down the hall and as Lexxa joined him, he pulled a hand cannon from his belt and quickly moved forward. Lexxa followed, her own eyes catching everything.

As destroyers went, the *Icarus* wasn't a big ship, but it packed a deadly punch, as it was built primarily to mount weapons. But it still held a shuttle bay and that bay housed three top-of-the-line FTL shuttles. That was their destination, although Lexxa didn't think they would ever get out of the *Icarus'* firing range before Woolston happily blew them up.

Unfortunately, it would never even get to that point. When the shuttle bay entry door opened, Captain David Woolston was waiting for them. He met Gregg Walko with a hard right cross that sent the tactical officer careening off the far wall. Stalking into the corridor, Captain Woolston went right after Lexxa, a murderous gleam in his eyes.

"I knew you wouldn't stay put," he snarled at her, hands clenched into fists.

Lexxa stepped back, falling quickly into a fighting stance. She cast a hurried glance at Walko, who was struggling to get back to his hands and knees. His eyes were glassy and Woolston paid him no mind at all, his own gaze fixed on Lexxa.

"I told them you were too much of a liability," he continued.

"Told who?" Lexxa asked, cautiously edging backward. Lexxa was strong, stronger than the average human. But there was something in Woolston's gaze that unsettled her. "I was only trying to keep you from murdering more people," she added, letting her anger lace her words with venom.

"You have no idea what's going on, Commander," Woolston chuckled. "Not a single bloody clue."

"Commander?" she questioned, narrowing her eyes at him. "You relieved me of my duties, Captain. Remember?"

"Old habits, I guess," he shrugged and surged forward.

Lexxa side-stepped the move, intending to catch him in the gut with her knee, but Woolston reversed himself so quickly, she barely even saw the backhand swing that caught her across the shoulder and sent her sprawling to the deck. Moving like a cat, Woolston was on her in a heartbeat, raining blows down on her.

"I never liked you," he seethed, cracking her across the jaw with a solid punch. "It's time you knew that you've never been anything more than a tool."

Lexxa struggled, trying to buck Woolston off her, but he seemed to be inhumanly strong and resisted her attempt to unseat him. He hit her again, harder this time, and stars erupted behind her eyes.

"And now you'll die, never realizing what could have been!" he growled, hitting her a third time. He raised his fist high, intending to finish her, when Walko clubbed him from behind and slammed him into the bulkhead.

Woolston quickly got back to his knees, shaking his head. His forehead was split from where it had impacted the wall, but instead of blood running down his face, a smoky mist began rising from it. Walko didn't hesitate and drove his knee into his captain's face with all his strength, slamming the man backward into the wall once again. But instead of the fight being over, Woolston simply shook his head and pulled himself to his feet, a maniacal grin on his face.

"I'm going to enjoy tearing you apart," he said icily, his gaze now fixed on Walko. "Literally."

But Walko lowered his shoulder and drove himself forward, lifting Woolston off the deck and propelling them both through the door and into the hanger bay. Woolston brought both his fists down hard, hammering into the back of Walko's neck and sending them both sprawling. Walko tried to climb to his feet, but he was still groggy and stumbled to his knees. Woolston was already up and returned the knee shot, sending the lieutenant spinning across the deck, nose broken and blood running freely.

In the corridor, Lexxa shakily pulled herself to her feet. Leaning heavily on the wall, she looked up, long enough to see Captain Woolston reach down and with one hand, grasp her friend by the throat and lift him high in the air. Walko's feet kicked feebly as Woolston held him aloft, crushing his throat with an iron grip that was impossible for a normal human. As Walko's eyes began to flutter and close, Lexxa heard the audible crack of neck bones and her friend suddenly went limp.

Just like that, Gregg Walko was dead.

Woolston carelessly tossed the body aside and turned back toward her, a look of absolute insanity on his face. A crack had appeared on his forehead, running down across his eye and cheek. Where blood should have been, Lexxa should only see oily smoke seeping from the wound. At that moment, she knew that her captain was truly gone. Keeping her eyes locked with his, she palmed the control pad and activated the door. It slid shut and she heard the locking mechanism engage.

Woolston's grin disappeared and he stepped toward the door, his eyes gleaming with hate. "You can't keep me in here, Lexxa," he snarled.

"I don't intend to," she said softly, her hands moving across the pad, keying in the sequence and her commander's safety override code.

Woolston realized what she was doing a moment too late. The shuttle door began to open, the bay depressurizing almost immediately. She saw only the captain's eyes go wide with surprise, before he was sucked backward toward the void of space. His body ricocheted off one of the shuttles, sending him pin wheeling through the air and then he was gone, blown into space along with the body of her friend.

Lexxa bowed her head, tears in her eyes. Walko was dead, savagely murdered by the captain, by a man that seemed no longer human. Shaking her head, she cleared her thoughts, knowing she had to focus now or all would be lost. "Computer," she said. "What is my official designation?"

"You are currently assigned as first officer aboard the *Icarus*," the toneless female voice replied.

Lexxa felt a small smile of victory pass her face, grateful that Woolston hadn't officially logged her dismissal yet. This would make things a little easier. "Computer, this is a delta-one intruder emergency," she went on. "Lock out all primary ship functions and bridge control on my command."

"Affirmative."

"Shut down all lifts and lock all doors apart from allowing me access to the bridge from my current location. Lockout parameters are to remain in place, with restoration possible only by my voice command or the voice command of Captain David Woolston."

"Affirmative."

"Engage."

"Primary ship functions are now locked down," the computer said. "Restoration on voice command of acting First Officer or Captain."

Nodding, she felt a slight measure of control creeping back into her. She could have bypassed allowing Woolston to end the lockdown, but that would have required more time and several other protocols that she didn't have time for. Besides, it wasn't like Woolston was going to come back from where she'd sent him.

Reaching down, she swept up Walko's dropped weapon and proceeded toward the bridge. Her would-be executioner was dead, but she wasn't out of the woods yet. She had a crew to deal with, a crew that would have likely been happy to see her dead, as well. The trick now was to avoid any more loss of life, including her own. With luck, she might have one more ally to depend on. She had to. It would be her only chance.

58

Chapter 7

Icarus

Trigani System, Confederation Space

Lexxa arrived on the bridge two minutes later, her hand cannon held before her. As she expected, there was turmoil on the bridge and quite a bit of angry shouting. The only one who wasn't shouting was Jirin, who was calmly seated in the command chair, listening to three other bridge officers demanding that he do something. For Lexxa, that was a good thing and she felt her chances of survival growing.

As she entered, weapon out, all eyes turned to her and the shouting ceased. She thought she caught a small trace of a smile on Jirin's face, before it quickly vanished beneath his trademark cool exterior. The others, though, were less than pleased to see her and even angrier at seeing a weapon in her hands, pointed at them.

"Computer" she said, raising a hand to silence their questions. "Access corridor H security footage playback from five minutes ago, as well that of the hanger deck."

"Completed," the computer said immediately.

"Run both feeds on the main bridge screen, side-by-side."

"Affirmative."

When the others began to object, she merely pointed to the screen and watched with satisfaction as they witnessed the attack unfold. She noticed their support of Captain Woolston begin to fade to wide-eyed shock and anger as they watched him murder Gregg Walko. They might not like her all that much, but Walko was a friend to everyone. And Captain Woolston had killed him in cold blood.

When the feeds were terminated, one of them turned to her, his face ashen. "Is this a trick?"

"No trick," she answered, her voice calm, but firm. "I am now acting captain of the *Icarus*. How long that remains will depend on what happens with FleetCom. But in the meantime, we all need to talk."

"That was my friend," the same officer spoke up, his voice angry. Doctor Daniel Fishman was the chief surgeon aboard the *Icarus* and probably Woolston's closest friend. Lexxa knew he wouldn't take this well at all.

"Captain Woolston was your friend," she corrected, her own voice soft. "He was also my friend, one of the few that I have had and one of the only people I trusted."

"And you killed him."

"I killed someone…or something, masquerading as the captain," she said evenly. "You saw the footage. That was not Captain Woolston."

"You were relieved of command by the captain," Fishman went on, sputtering now. He was reaching for something, anything that would bolster his argument, but nothing was there.

"Captain Woolston did not log my termination," she stated. "Perhaps he hoped I would come to my senses. Or perhaps he simply meant to kill me and could more easily explain my death if I had not been officially relieved of duty. Whatever the case, I am now in command of the *Icarus* and will remain so until someone tells me otherwise."

"And what if we refuse to follow orders?" Fishman said, although there was not much steam left in his anger. He seemed deflated, almost without hope.

"There are FTL shuttles in the hanger bay," she answered. "As I understand that this situation is shocking and without explanation, anyone that is not comfortable with my taking command of the *Icarus* is welcome to leave. There will be no actions logged against anyone that does so, either."

"And you?" Lieutenant Akashi asked skeptically, as if he was able to read her thoughts. "Are you just going to take the ship and flee from FleetCom?"

"That was actually the mission we were carrying out," she said, trying to keep the smugness out of her voice. She knew that beyond her and Woolston, the crew didn't know the specifics of their mission. Even she didn't apparently know it all, according to Woolston. To say she was uncertain about the waters she was getting ready to sail into was an understatement.

"What are you talking about?" Fishman asked.

Sighing, Lexxa pointed to the ready room. "We have a lot to talk about." Turning to Jirin, she nodded appreciatively at him. "Can I trust you?" was all that she asked.

"I follow the commanding officer of this ship," he stated flatly. "I saw Captain Woolston die in a tragic shuttle bay accident. That makes you the acting captain of this vessel until, as you said, someone tells you otherwise."

She smiled and handed the weapon to him, which he took hesitantly, then attached it to his belt. "Computer," she said. "The delta-one intruder emergency is still in effect. Keep all ship-wide lockdown protocols in place, but restore helm control to the bridge.”

“Affirmative.”

“Activate cloaking device and get us out of here, Jirin,” she said softly, before turning to follow the others to the ready room.

“Heading, Commander?” Jirin asked as he slid into the helmsman’s chair.

“Anywhere but here for the moment,” she answered, looking at stars of deep space on the screen. “We need some time to sort things out.”

“Yes, Commander,” he answered, his hands moving over the controls. Moments later, the destroyer vanished under her cloak.

“Oh, and Jirin?”

He looked at her and she merely tapped her ear. He nodded immediately and went back to his board.

“Are you going to tell us what this is all about?” Fishman asked as she walked into the ready room. None of the three were sitting and they all looked ready for a fight.

“Yes, who was that if it wasn’t really the captain?” Commander Zorn asked, his visage thoughtful. Charles Zorn was the only science officer aboard the *Icarus*, so it automatically made him a member of the senior staff. Zorn was always quiet and thoughtful, polite to a point when he spoke. But he was on edge now and Lexxa couldn’t blame him.

“Please, sit,” she said, taking her own seat and then looking at them all expectantly. She was silent until finally they each sat, Fishman sitting last and doing so with a loud, exasperated sigh.

"With the captain and Walko gone, we're all that's left of the senior staff," Lexxa began. "I want to start with you and then I'll speak to the crew."

"What about Jirin?"

"Someone has to fly the ship," she tried to be light-hearted, but knew she failed. These were dark times for all of them. Still, she knew Jirin was listening as she had instructed him to. They didn't need to know that, though, because she wanted their unvarnished opinion about whether they would accept her as temporary captain.

"So, what do you intend to do?" Fishman pressed.

Lexxa sighed and cleared her throat. "I'm not sure what Captain Woolston told you about our mission, but there is much more to it than probably what you, or even I, currently know."

"We went into a wargames battle and were attacked," Fishman said, leaning forward. "What's not to know?"

Lexxa looked at Akashi. He had been on the bridge, so knew firsthand what had actually happened. Fishman and Zorn had not been, so they only knew what they were told. She hoped Akashi would speak up, but he remained silent, his face a mask of stone.

"We were not attacked," she explained after several tense moments. "It was the *Icarus* who did the attacking. We were the sole aggressors."

"What are you saying?" Zorn demanded, his normally calm demeanor showing cracks.

"Lieutenant?" she pressed, looking at Akashi.

"The commander speaks the truth," he said flatly, meeting her gaze without flinching. "We attacked the *Nottingham* and the *Dominant*."

"What the hell for?" Fishman burst out.

"Captain Woolston was under orders to take the *Icarus* from FleetCom control," she answered, grateful that she had gotten that much out of Akashi. "There is a growing schism within the Confederation and the *Icarus* is part of an attempt to fix everything that is wrong with us right now."

"You mean a coup d'état?"

"Something like that," she nodded. "However, something went wrong."

"You think?" Fishman snapped. "Our captain is dead and you're practically pulling a mutiny!"

Lexxa ignored the outburst. "I was privy to orders that instructed us to disable the *Nottingham* and that the *Dominant* had crew members on board that would knock out her power, allowing us to safely take the *Icarus*. No blood was to be shed."

"Then why did we destroy the *Nottingham*?" It was Akashi that asked and Lexxa could tell that despite the cool exterior, he was actually pretty broken up about what had happened. She took that as a good sign.

"I don't know," she shrugged helplessly. "I opposed it, but Captain Woolston had his orders, I guess."

"And who was giving these orders?" Fishman asked sharply.

Lexxa paused, looking at each of them in turn before answering. "Sector 6 gave us the original orders."

"I knew it," the doctor spat. "They would have to be behind the murder of so many.”

“I disagree,” Lexxa countered, ignoring the surgeon’s glare. “I believe Sector 6’s ultimate goal is to rid the Confederation and FleetCom of corruption, nothing more.”

“By killing innocents?”

“By taking a next generation battleship out of the hands of people that would use it for the wrong reasons,” she said, glaring back at Fishman now and backing him down. “The *Icarus* and the *Dominant* represent a new phase in FleetCom and there was concern that the wargames testing was meant to signify a shift in the balance of power,” she went on. “Our orders were to blunt that by taking the *Icarus* and removing the temptation to use it unjustly.”

“And in the process, a starship was destroyed with all hands lost,” Fishman said bitterly, refusing to let go of his anger.

“That’s why I think there’s more to this than any of us know,” Lexxa said. “There has to be a third player in all of this. Captain Woolston’s actions were completely out of character for him and well outside of the orders we were originally given. And you saw what he was before he died!”

“You still think Sector 6 is not behind this?” Zorn asked.

“I honestly don’t know what to think at the moment,” she answered. “But I have a contact in Sector 6 who I intend to ask.”

“Well, I can’t be a party to this,” Fishman said, shaking his head. Looking directly at Lexxa, he continued, still obviously angry. “I don’t believe you’re telling us everything and quite honestly, I’m not willing to serve under your command. Since you’re obviously hell-bent on taking the ship, I will take you up on your offer to leave.”

"Very well," Lexxa said, looking at the others. "And you two?"

"I am not at all comfortable with you taking orders from Sector 6," Zorn spoke up. "I will join the doctor."

"Akashi?"

He looked at her blankly and for a moment, Lexxa thought he might stay. After all, he had presided over the destruction of the *Khygan* and had to be looking for some reason to justify what he had done. "I will leave, as well," he finally said.

"Very well," she sighed in disappointment, standing up. "If you'll report to the shuttle bay and standby, you may have a few others joining you."

Without another word, all of them stood up and filed out of the room. Lexxa followed them slowly back onto the bridge, not at all surprised at the exodus, but still concerned about whether she would have anyone left to run the ship. As the trio then quickly departed, Lexxa looked at Jirin.

"Did you get everything?" she asked.

"Yes, Captain," Jirin replied. "I have also taken the liberty of alerting my contact in Sector 6 to rendezvous with the shuttles immediately upon departure."

"So you knew?" she asked, feeling some comfort at knowing that he probably did. It meant she might not have to be so alone in all of this.

"Yes, Captain," he replied. "I had my own orders to monitor the situation here. There was a grave concern that either you or Captain Woolston or both intended to go rogue."

"Kovok?" She guessed bitterly.

Jirin nodded.

"And your report?"

"I haven't given it, yet," he replied matter-of-factly. "But I believe you're as much a pawn in this whole game as the *Icarus* is."

"Well that's kind of a relief," she said humorlessly.

"If it's any consolation, I believe you," he added. "But there is a lot to consider at the moment, wouldn't you agree?"

"Completely," she sighed.

"What I do know is that we can't let those that are leaving get back to FleetCom right away, at least until we figure out what's going on."

"Agreed."

"Sector 6 has a transport inbound to Starbase 214," he said. "They will take on the shuttles there and take their time processing the crew back to earth space dock. That should allow them to keep things quiet and give them time to figure out who the third player is."

"Do you think there is one, Jirin?"

"Hard to say, but it's certainly possible."

"And you took care of the shuttles?" she asked, knowing already that he was probably way ahead of her.

"I have already disabled subspace communications in both shuttles and programmed a preplanned flight path," he answered. "Once they depart the *Icarus*, I will activate the autopilot. They will arrive at Starbase 214 safe and soundlessly and well behind Sector 6, who will be waiting for them."

"Well done," she said and then swung herself into her command chair. After a moment contemplating the stars streaking across the view screen, she keyed the comm button. "Attention all hands, this is your captain speaking."

68

Chapter 8

Dominant

Kabala Sector, Confederation Space

"Captain Rydan," Lieutenant Creer reported, looking up from her station. She was still pale and looked shaken, but had insisted on returning to duty. Rydan would have preferred she take some time to recover, but he knew he needed her, so had not objected when she returned to the bridge. "You have a priority one message coming through," she continued. "Eyes only."

Rydan sprang up from the command chair. "I'll take it in the ready room."

As the door slide shut behind up, he threw himself into his seat and keyed up his channel. He'd been sitting idle for nearly 36 hours now, awaiting new orders. FleetCom was in an upheaval and the deep ramifications of the *Icarus* destroying the *Nottingham* were growing deeper by the hour. He hated having to sit, but Doyle had informed him that he was to keep the *Dominant* where it was until she ordered him elsewhere. He had been waiting for her to contact him since that moment, so he was mildly surprised to see a former crewmate of his on the feed, one Takuya Akashi, speaking to him from what looked like a hanger bay. It only took a moment for it to fit together for him. The man was on the *Icarus*.

"Takuya," he exclaimed. "I haven't seen you in months. Why are…"

"Shut up and listen, Sykian," the man interrupted, speaking rapidly. "I only have a moment. We are leaving the *Icarus*."

"We?"

"Senior officers and other staff," Akashi went on. "Woolston is dead. Lexxa is in command."

"Wait, slow down! What on earth is happening on the ship?"

"No time, long story, not sure I have it all figured out myself," Akashi answered. "Lexxa has the *Icarus*, but no crew."

"Did she mutiny?"

"Uncertain what her role is in all of this, but Woolston went rogue first and was killed. She survived. Luck or planning, I don't know."

"Why are you telling me this?"

"Sector 6 is involved, too, but I don't know how deeply."

"Sector 6?" Rydan said incredulously. "Takuya, this is absurd! Do you realize how this sounds?"

"Listen, Sykian," the man said hurriedly. "I only know some of what's going on and not near enough to know who is behind all of this. I knew that Woolston was going to take the *Icarus*, but his actions against the *Nottingham* and your ship were well beyond what I expected. He was clearly working outside our original orders."

"Are you saying this was a coup?" Rydan asked, anger suddenly seeping into his voice. A lot of people had died when the *Icarus* had turned her weapons on their ships.

"It's exactly that, but I don't know how deep it goes," Akashi replied. "However, if Sector 6 gets to Lexxa, she'll disappear and maybe so will any chance FleetCom has of figuring out what's really going on here."

"And you're leaving?"

"I have to," Akashi answered, but offered nothing more.

"Where are you going?"

"We're taking FTL shuttles, but I'm certain that Sector 6 will be rolling out a red carpet for us somewhere," he said drily. "I'd be surprised if Lexxa hasn't contacted her controller and told them we are abandoning ship. They're not going to want us talking to anyone."

"How can you be sure?"

"Because something big is going down, Sykian," he answered. "Sector 6 is involved. FleetCom general is involved. And there may be another player, too, but I don't know who." The man paused, looking around, before looking back at the screen. "Others are here. I have to go. Find Lexxa. Get to the bottom of what's going on."

With that, the screen went dark.

Captain Rydan sat still, calmly looking at the blank screen, mulling over the man's words in his head. He and Akashi weren't exactly bosom buddies, but they knew each other well enough during their time serving aboard the *Cherokee*. When the *Cherokee* had gone in for a full refit and new command crew, he'd been assigned to the *Dominant* and Akashi went to the *Icarus*. And now here they were again, joined by a growing conflict that neither of them could hope to understand.

After several minutes and with a plan of his own beginning to form, he decided to contact Admiral Doyle. She'd told him before not to contact her directly, but this new information changed things drastically, at least in his mind. After getting past her irritation at him for disobeying her orders, he relayed what he knew and informed her that Lexxa was now sitting in the captain's chair of the *Icarus*.

"So, what's your course of action, captain?" Admiral Doyle finally asked after silently pondering his report for several long moments.

"She might have the *Icarus*, but according to Akashi, she needs a crew," Rydan answered thoughtfully. "And she certainly isn't going to go through FleetCom channels to request one."

"Agreed. And your point is?"

"I've been around a long time," he said, referring to his race's ability to live for centuries. "If she's after a crew, she's going to look where spacers and freighter captains are hanging out. That means she'll go completely off the grid."

"You know where she might go?"

"I can hazard a guess, Admiral," Rydan replied. "There's an asteroid belt beyond Starbase 82, deep in unclaimed space. It's unofficially known as Rockfleet."

"Rockfleet," Doyle repeated. "I'm not familiar with it. What is it?"

"A huge asteroid, home to a place called Conways. It's kind of your standard out-of-the-way spacer bar, but totally lawless."

"Lovely," Doyle sighed, wincing and rubbing her forehead. "Are you familiar with it?"

"I know of it," Rydan explained, "but I have never had the need to become a patron."

"Do you think she'd go to those lengths?"

"While we have been waiting, I've taken the liberty of studying the profile info for the command crew of the *Icarus*," he said. "Including Lexxa. While a lot of her past is classified, she's had some scraps with FleetCom and the law in general, before Sector 6 reined her in. If she has indeed taken the *Icarus* and there is a FleetCom coup in progress, she's going to go to the deepest hole she can find right now."

"And this Conways is it?"

"It's not a hotel bar," Rydan said drily. "And it's the closest place she'll be able to find what she needs."

"Well, at the moment, I don't have anything better," Doyle replied after thinking over what he was proposing. "I don't have to tell you that we're in a world of trouble here."

"If I may, what is the status in FleetCom right now? We are understandably in the dark out here."

"Most of us are still in the dark, Captain," she answered truthfully, "but this is what we know. FleetCom general is in an upheaval and believes Sector 6 is complicit. Seems as if Woolston has a deep past with them and that's got a lot of people very upset. Sector 6 won't say much beyond proposing the idea that there is something much deeper at work within the Confederation and Woolston went completely off the grid with his actions."

"But Sector 6 is part of FleetCom."

"You would think so," she sighed, "and no one has the slightest clue how to start untangling all of this. Right now, it's a huge mess and the sooner we recover the *Icarus* and bring in Lexxa or whoever is commanding the ship, the closer we'll be to finding our answers."

"Understood, ma'am," Rydan said with a nod. "Orders?"

"Proceed at your best guess right now, Captain," Doyle instructed him. "If you believe Lexxa might be heading off the grid, I'll give you full latitude to find and intercept her."

"And if we succeed?"

"I would hope she'd give up peacefully, Captain, but she's

commanding one of the most dangerous ships in the quadrant, second only to your own. If she's gone rogue and decides to fight, you'll be in for a rough ride, even with the *Dominant* at your disposal. What is your current operational status, anyway?"

"We are fully operational," Rydan answered. "The main bridge has been sealed off and will need a full space dock crew to repair her. But for now, we're operating from the battle bridge with no loss of efficiency."

"Excellent," Doyle said. "Keep me apprised of the situation on my personal secure channel."

"Yes, ma'am."

"And Captain?" she added. "Be careful out there. My gut tells me this is deeper than any of us know."

"Yes, ma'am," Rydan repeated.

"Doyle out."

The screen went dark and Sykian Rydan leaned back in his chair, steepling his fingers together in thought. Two days ago, he was an officer on the bridge of a state-of-the-art Confederation battlecruiser. Now he was commanding it, getting ready to go after someone commanding a vessel that was nearly as dangerous as his own. Coming out of this with everyone intact and no more loss of life seemed remote, at best.

Clenching his jaw, he keyed his comm. "Helm," he said, "set a course for the Mordan system, maximum speed."

"Yes, sir," came the reply.

With a sigh, Captain Rydan stood up from his chair. "Here we go," he said quietly.

Chapter 9

Icarus

Trigani System, Confederation Space

Lexxa slipped into the captain's quarters—her quarters now—and fell into the chair sitting before the desk. She looked blankly at the darkened screen and at the few items surrounding it, items that reminded her of Captain Woolston, a man she had once enjoyed serving under. A man who she had thought was her friend, at least before he told her she had been nothing more than a tool for his use. Pushing away the melancholy thoughts, she activated the system. "Computer, establish priority one connection. Contact Zero Delta Three Omni Delta Nine," she said, reciting Kovok's personal security code.

"Connection established." The computer recited.

It took less than ten seconds before the screen lit up, showing the face of a man that she both respected and often hated. Kovok was the face of Sector 6, the Confederation's security organization that had made her younger life a living hell. Over the years, she'd had to constantly remind herself that Kovok was never a part of the horrors that she had endured when she was younger, nor was he responsible for the disappearance of her mother.

Upon his assignment to the covert organization, Kovok had worked hard to repair what had been done to her in the past, even going so far as to share with her everything that he knew about her.

Her birth, the genetic experimentation that had led to her existence, and most importantly, her father. Because of Kovok, a lot of her questions had been answered. It was also because of him that she was in FleetCom today.

For years after she had escaped Sector 6, she had lived on the edge of space, plying her way with smugglers and raiders in the veritable underbelly of the galaxy. One day, fortune, or lack thereof, had resulted in her vessel running afoul of a Confederation cruiser and she had been captured along with the rest of the crew. At that time, she was no more than a spacer, a peon aboard a freight runner making highly illegal transactions. Her captain and most of the vessel's officers had earned some hefty penitentiary time and she likely would have been given the same.

But that's when Kovok intervened and rescued her from certain incarceration. Still, she spent the better part of six months in his presence, being told everything he knew about who she was and where she had come from. Much of it, her mother had told her when she was younger. But Kovok filled in a lot of the blanks, and in doing so, had fostered a rage in her she had never known. The biggest reason for that was his lack of knowledge when it came to her mother. Lexxa had never known whether her mother had lived or died and unfortunately, it was before Kovok's time in Sector 6. He did not know, either, nor had he been able to find out. But in exchange for her enlisting in FleetCom and becoming an asset of Sector 6, he would do everything in his power to continue the search. So far, that had amounted to nothing and Lexxa was well aware of the animosity growing within her.

"Is your connection secure, commander?" Kovok asked in that

maddeningly calm tone of his.

"I wouldn't be contacting you if it wasn't," she replied, her voice clipped. "I trust you're aware of what happened?"

"I am aware that a Confederation battlecruiser has been destroyed with all hands lost," Kovok said and Lexxa caught what she thought was a glimmer of anger in his tone. But it softened immediately. He wasn't holding her responsible for it. "Jirin has given me a full report," he added.

"Woolston went rogue," she explained. "There was nothing I could do to stop him."

"Nothing?"

"Believe me, I tried, sir," she said. "I ended up in the brig because of it and only minutes from being airlocked, before a friend gave his life to save me."

Kovok was silent for a moment, before saying, "I understand. What is your current status?"

"I have taken command of the *Icarus*. Most of the crew has decided they don't want to play in this game and have requested immediate leave of absence."

"Yes, Jirin informed me," Kovok nodded. "We will, of course, intercept them at Starbase 214 and keep them safe."

"And silent," Lexxa added knowingly, her tone a little sharper than she intended.

"The longer we can keep a lid on this, the better chance we have of discovering who Woolston was working for."

"I'm guessing it wasn't Sector 6?"

"Only so far as what you knew," Kovok answered. "Nothing ever changed on our end and we certainly never issued orders to murder a starship crew."

"I wish I could believe that."

"I assure you, that order never came from Sector 6." If he was offended at her statement, he didn't show it.

"What do you need me to do?" she snapped.

"I'm afraid you'll need to take on some new crew members, commander," he answered. "You cannot survive with the skeleton crew you currently have."

"You might not like the people I pick, Kovok," she stated flatly. "Anyone I sign on will not have conventional FleetCom credentials."

"Quite honestly, I cannot think of a better idea right now," Kovok answered. "I do not anticipate you are going to get out of this in one piece, so you will to need some unconventional help. FleetCom is mobilizing two hunter-killer fleets and the *Dominant* is already actively searching for you."

"Have you tried to convince anyone of what's really going on?"

"We have," Kovok countered, "not that it has made much difference. The growing void between FleetCom general and Sector 6 is becoming difficult, perhaps impossible, to traverse anymore. And the Confederation itself is having a hard time trusting either of us."

"Very well," she said. "Do you have a contingency plan?"

"As much as we can," he answered with a nod. "I will send you coordinates for a rendezvous. It's quite some distance from you and we need to be careful. It'll take time to prepare on our end."

"For what?"

"This has the potential to explode into a civil war, Captain,"

Kovok explained. "If we do not play our cards right, we could be looking at the end of the Confederation."

"Isn't that what Woolston was trying to jumpstart by destroying the *Nottingham*?"

"That's our thought, yes," he answered. "And while I'm sorry that you're in the middle of this, I put you on that ship to be my eyes and ears."

"And look what it got me."

"Despite what you might think, you've done more good than you realize," Kovok said, his voice quieter. "With Woolston dead, you have forced our enemies to change their strategy. They lost a key asset in Woolston and they also lost his ship. They have to be in disarray."

"We can hope," she said, then lowered her head. She suddenly realized that she was so tired. "Kovok?"

"Yes?"

"I didn't want any of this to happen," she said, her voice halting.

"I realize that, but unfortunately many others do not," he replied. "What has happened was beyond your control, but you are in control now. We will find a way to turn this to our advantage and against our enemy, whoever they might be."

Lexxa nodded, but said nothing.

"Is there something else?" Kovok asked, one eyebrow rising in question.

For a moment, Lexxa considered telling him about her nightmares, but quickly thought better of it. Let Kovok deal with what he already knows. No point in sharing more of her frailties with him.

"No, sir," she said quietly. "Relay the coordinates. I'll ensure we make the rendezvous."

"And Lexxa?" Kovok added, his own voice low.

"What?"

"I would guard against telling anyone."

"Not many people left onboard and only one that I trust," she replied, failing to keep the bitterness out of her voice.

"Nevertheless, for the time being, eyes only."

"What about Jirin?"

"No," Kovok shook his head. "Right now, there is too much at stake."

"Understood," Lexxa said, her eyes downcast. She was already feeling the pressure. Not being able to confide in Jirin would make things more difficult. But she had to believe Kovok had his reasons. She just hoped they were good ones. "Lexxa out."

The screen went dark and she waited. Several moments later, a printed message scrolled across the darkened screen. It was in code, and a few commands entered into the control board, decoded it. She had her coordinates. And something else.

Getting a crew onboard was more important now than ever.

Chapter 10

Icarus

Tyrus System, Free Space

Lexxa stared at the blade, her eyes focusing on the bead of blood slowly running the length of the knife's edge. The Admiral lay dead at her feet, his throat slashed, but she didn't know why. Had she killed him? Was she somehow responsible?

Finish it.

Those words. Whispered in the darkness of her mind. She had heard them before. Spoken to her by…who?

Finish it, Lexxa. Complete your mission.

Her head seemed to spin and she felt herself raising the blade to her face. The dagger's point grew larger. Perfect to finish the job. Just a little push and it would be over. Her mission would be over. And her mother. Her mother would finally be safe.

Yes, she thought. This was the only way.

The chime, normally so innocuous and unobtrusive, cut through her tortured mind. She sat up, sucking in her breath as reality quickly began to reset itself within her. The dagger was gone. The Admiral was gone. And she was in her bunk, sitting up and feeling a drop of cold sweat running down her cheek.

Her door chimed again and she looked up. "Lights," she croaked, bringing up the lighting in her quarters. How long had she been asleep? Looking at the chronometer next to her bed, she groaned, realizing she'd been asleep for less than two hours. Two hours in the past forty-eight. That was going to get her killed if she kept it up.

The chime sounded again and Lexxa shook her head, feeling the headache of stress and over-exertion beginning to creep into her brain. She swung her feet over the side of the bed and pressed her fist to her temple. "Come," she finally said, feeling the pain begin to recede slightly, if even for a little bit.

The door slid open and Lexxa looked up as a young crew member entered her quarters. Head down, hands folded in front of her, Lexxa had seen her before but didn't know her name.

"I'm sorry, Captain," the woman said softly. "I wasn't aware you were taking rack time. I can come back later."

"No, that's okay," Lexxa replied, knowing that had she continued sleeping, she would have ended up killing herself. Again. Her nightmares never ended any other way. She always killed The Admiral and then herself. Only then could she guarantee the safety of her mother. At least that's what the dreams told her. "What do you need?"

The young woman stood at attention, her angular features catching the light, her large eyes seemingly worried.

"Relax," Lexxa offered, waving a hand easily in the air to put the crew member at ease.

"I'm sorry, ma'am," she said.

Lexxa shook her head. "Just Captain will do," she corrected. "At least for now."

"Captain."

"Better."

"I just…I just wanted a moment to talk with you," the woman said. "I wanted to tell you that I support you in all of this and I would like to help, if possible."

"Well, that's nice to hear," Lexxa chuckled humorlessly. "There's not a lot of you left. Unfortunately, that doesn't leave me with much of a ringing endorsement."

"I understand," the woman nodded. "But I believe in you. And I can pilot a ship."

"You're a helmsman?" Lexxa asked, looking up expectantly.

"Well, kind of."

"Just kind of?" Lexxa cocked an eyebrow.

"My parents ran a trade organization from Bazanti," the young woman replied. "They had an old lotus-class freighter that I helmed for a couple years before entering FleetCom."

"And your FleetCom training was on helming a starship?"

"Actually, I'm in security," she answered, her eyes quickly downcast again, as if the admission embarrassed her.

"Well…" Lexxa began, pausing to look at the woman, waiting for her to fill in the blank.

"Ronara," she answered, understanding the pause. "Ensign Ronara."

"Well, Ensign Ronara," Lexxa cleared her throat. "So, you're a security officer with helm capabilities."

"Yes, Captain."

"Are you familiar with the *Icarus*?

"Yes, Captain," Ronara said, brightening. "I trained on the helm simulators at the academy every chance I got."

Lexxa leaned back on her bunk, looking the young woman up and down. She was young and certainly attractive, but she lacked conviction in her words. "Ronara," she said after a few moments. "You said you're from Bazanti, correct?"

"Yes."

"I imagine you were training in Psy-Ops at the academy, as well, were you not?"

"Yes, Captain," she answered, seemingly embarrassed.

"There are not many people from your planet in FleetCom and most of those are psychic operatives with Sector 6. Any particular reason why you ended up in security?"

Ronara shook her head, eyes again going to the floor. "It's…it's hard to explain," she answered. "I'm not very good at the psychic connection like everyone else from my planet. It's always been a struggle for me. That's why my parents put me on the freighter. At least that was something I was good at."

"So you thought security was the answer to your perceived failings?"

Ronara shrugged. "I guess."

"Well, Ronara," Lexxa sighed. "I'm not in a position to be picky, nor am I in much need of security. The *Icarus* is a small ship as it is and I have precious few crew members left."

"Does that mean you have no need of me?" Ronara asked, her voice cracking a bit as the specter of being put off the ship began to loom before her.

"Nothing of the sort," Lexxa answered, rising to her feet and ignoring the swell of pain in her head. She placed a reassuring hand on the young woman's shoulder and offered her a smile. "Report to the bridge, Lieutenant."

"I'm just an ensign, Captain," Ronara corrected.

"As of this moment, you're a lieutenant," Lexxa said, still smiling. "If we get out of this and I don't end up locked up for the next twenty years, I'll do my best to make it permanent."

"Yes, Captain," Ronara said with a nod, her countenance quickly brightening.

"Begin familiarizing yourself with the helm controls," Lexxa continued. "I have no idea what is going to happen in the next few days or weeks, but I want a competent crew member at the helm of the *Icarus*."

"Yes, Captain," Ronara said again. "And, thank you."

Lexxa just nodded and watched as the young woman turned and exited her quarters, a noticeable spring in her step. It was her first meeting with one of the few remaining crew members of the *Icarus*. If Ronara was competent, it would make things much easier for her and Jirin. And while she had no crystal ball to tell her how things were going to end up, she knew she would need the best people she could get if they were to stay ahead of their enemies. That thought brought up another, much more disconcerting one.

Who were their enemies?

With her luck, probably everybody.

With a resolute sigh, she exited her quarters and headed toward the bridge. She wouldn't get any more sleep, that much she knew. At least she would be spared the nightmare for a little while.

86

Chapter II

Icarus

Mordan System, Free Space

"Position." Lexxa said grimly, her hands gripping the rails of her captain's chair. In front of her, Ronara was piloting the *Icarus*, moving the agile destroyer through the asteroid field. It wasn't something that Lexxa would normally be comfortable putting in the hands of an inexperienced helmsman, but Ronara had proven herself to be a woman of her word—she was actually a pretty fair pilot. Still, Lexxa's muscles were tense as she watched the asteroids move past the ship at a speed somewhere north of her comfort level.

"Heading one three three, mark six," Ronara answered crisply, her hands smoothly working her control board. "We will be in comm range inside of five minutes."

"I show two vessels on sensors," Jirin spoke up. "One is a freighter broadcasting a Sol port transponder."

"The other?" Lexxa asked, knowing it wasn't going to be good news.

"Rigellian destroyer, predator-class," he replied cautiously.

"That's a mean ship," Lexxa mused thoughtfully. "What's it doing out here?"

"Unknown, Captain," Jirin answered plainly. "Passive scan shows normal power readings. She's not geared up for battle."

"That could change quickly enough. If it gets ugly, how ready are we?"

"Cloaking device is fully active, Captain," he replied matter-of-factly, looking up at her briefly as if she was insane. After all, there were only three of them on the bridge and only two crew members down in engineering. If they ran into any serious trouble…well, he didn't want to think about what the outcome would be. "I would strongly advise against decloaking," he added.

"Well, I'm certainly not looking to court a Rigellian captain for dinner," she replied sourly. "We'll have to get in a different way. Transfer comm control to me."

Jirin's hands ran across his board. "Comm control to you, Captain."

Lexxa brushed the control screen and keyed in a communication code she had stored in her head for years. She hadn't used it in a while; hadn't needed to since Kovok and Sector 6 forced her onto the path of righteousness, as she not so fondly remembered. When her board showed an open connection, she spoke quickly. "Alpha Nine Zeta on approach vector one three three, mark six," she said crisply. "Looking for the Motel Manager."

There were several audible beeps over the comm system, before a female voice answered with one word. "Lexxa?"

"Callahan," she said with relief. "Good to hear your voice."

"Lexxa," the woman replied over the comm. "How long has it been? I heard you straightened up and started flying right."

"Long story, Brenna. I'm inbound. Can you clear a transport pad?"

"What, you don't want to bring your ship inside?"

"I'd prefer not to," Lexxa replied. "We're hot and I don't like the look of that cruiser sitting outside your front door."

"Oh, you mean Dra'ag's ship."

"The Rigellian destroyer?"

"That's the one," Callahan replied. "Captain Dra'ag's got a beef with a Krayht trader who's due in sometime in the next week. I told him if he opens fire inside Rockfleet, I'm taking his ship. So he opted to wait by the front door."

Lexxa breathed a sigh of relief. "Glad he's not looking for me," she said.

"Any particular reason he would be?"

"Like I said, we're a little hot. I'd prefer to keep my ship out of anyone's vision right now."

"Understood," Callahan said after a moment. "I'll relay the coordinates to you. Just yourself?"

"Yes."

"Give me five minutes."

"I'll need about ten," Lexxa replied. "We're still inbound and flying with a skeleton crew."

"Ten it is."

"Lexxa out."

The comm was cut and Jirin immediately spoke up. "Captain, my sensors picked up the comm signal emanating from that rather large asteroid. I am not familiar with this sector. I take it there's a base on the surface?"

"Inside, to be specific," Lexxa replied. "Place called Conways."

"Conways," Jirin repeated. "I've never heard of it."

"I'm not surprised," she said. "Not many FleetCom personnel

know of it and far fewer know where it's located. It's about as ungovernable a place as you'll find, which is one of the reasons it's outside Confederation space."

"And you're going to take on a crew from there?"

"Conways has some of the best spacers and crew members you'll find," she answered. "If the price is right, you can get someone halfway competent. If they're desperate, you'll do even better."

"You've been here before?" Ronara spoke up.

"In another life," Lexxa said almost wistfully.

"Do you trust this Callahan?" Jirin asked.

"You don't trust anyone you run across at Conways," she said evenly. "That tends to get one killed. Or worse."

Jirin nodded, but said nothing. If he had any reservations about what she was going to do, he kept it to himself. Lexxa didn't blame him. She had her own reservations about coming here. But as far as she was concerned, she didn't think she had any other options.

"Coordinates coming through, Captain," Jirin announced after several silent minutes.

"Bring us around to the far side of the asteroid," Lexxa instructed Ronara as she stood up. "Hold station while I'm inside."

"Captain," Jirin said, looking up. "Do you think this could be a trap?"

"I always think that," she said. "Hopefully, I'm wrong this time."

"This time?"

"As I said, long story," she replied, offering him a half smile. "I'll tell you about it someday."

"That doesn't instill me with a lot of confidence."

"Relax, Jirin. I'll be fine."

"And if not?"

"Then the *Icarus* is yours," she answered after a brief pause. "If that happens, then my advice would be to try to get in contact with Kovok."

"Any particular reason why you haven't done that yet yourself?"

"Because I trust him even less than Brenna Callahan," she lied and walked toward the lift. "Jirin, you have the conn. Maintain cloak and comm silence," she went on. "I'll try to wrap things up quickly."

"Yes, Captain," he said, sliding out of his seat and taking his place in her command chair.

Lexxa didn't look back and hurried to the transporter room. Miraculously, there was a crewman staffing the pad, working on maintenance. She recognized him and gave him a friendly nod. "Ensign Bobek," she said. "Glad to see you manning a station."

"Thank you, Captain," he said graciously, stepping up to the transporter controls. He was one of the few crew members that had remained on board when Lexxa had given everyone the option to stay or leave, putting his faith in her when few others had. "No regrets," he added with a genuine smile.

"Good to hear," she said, stepping up onto the pad. "For all our sakes, I'll do my best to make things right."

"I know that, Captain," he nodded appreciatively. "Coordinates?"

"Jirin just transferred them down."

Bobek looked at them and then cast a concerned glance back up to Lexxa. "Those coordinates are directly inside the asteroid we are orbiting."

"I know," she offered him a knowing smile. "Happily, not all things are as they appear, Ensign. Energize."

"Yes, ma'am," he said, returning her smile. A moment later, Lexxa disappeared in the swirl of transport energy.

She materialized on a single pad, run by a grubby looking spacer whose tunic was stained pretty much from top to bottom with drink and other things Lexxa preferred not to guess. He grunted at her and then turned his attention back to a holo chess board sitting on his console.

Lexxa paid him no mind and exited the transporter room, stepping directly into the bar. It was a large, one-room establishment filled with all manner of humans and aliens, most of them rowdy and all of them drinking.

A woman made her way through the knot of people toward Lexxa, elbowing aside those that pressed in on her or failed to move in the first place. Brenna Callahan was a former spacer, a hard worker and ruthless business woman. With funding from a source she preferred not to name, she had taken over the seedy space bar from a former business partner after he had been killed when raiders hit his luxury space yacht. There was still much speculation on whether or not that tragedy had been carefully arranged or not, but no one had ever dared to accuse Brenna outright. To her own credit, she had never done anything to dissuade the rumors, either. Whether it was true or not, no one could argue with the benefit of people fearing what you were capable of.

"Lexxa," Brenna greeted, running a hand through her striking red hair and pushing it away from her face. Brenna was fond of telling people about her Earth Irish ancestry and capped it off by telling people she had also inherited their temper, so people should watch their step around her. That, at least, Lexxa agreed with. She had seen Brenna Callahan angry and it was something she would rather not be on the receiving end of, despite her own formidable skills.

"Brenna," Lexxa returned the greeting, clasping the bar owner's forearm. "It's been a long time."

"You're not still mad about what happened, are you?" Brenna asked, a small smile tugging at the corners of her mouth.

"As long as I never find out that you profited off it, then we're square," Lexxa answered, but she had no returning smile. The memories weren't pleasant, but they hadn't resulted in any lasting damage. Several years prior to her entry into FleetCom, when she was a hotshot smuggler in her own right, several Krayht 'businessmen' had arranged to have some mercenaries kidnap her in order to sell her into slavery. It was not the kind of slavery where work was required, either, and that, above anything, had infuriated Lexxa. Her ancestry had paid dividends that time and when she was done, her captors were dead and she had airlocked the captain into deep space before bartering her way off the vessel.

For a while afterward, she had cast a wary eye toward Brenna Callahan, since the kidnapping had taken place in Conways. But she never had any way to prove that the bar owner had been behind the ease of which the kidnappers had broken into her locked room. So the accusations remained more or less unspoken, although Brenna had assured her she had never had anything to do with it. Still, Lexxa always had an eye toward any subterfuge when she was around Conways, and more importantly, Brenna Callahan.

Brenna led her through the packed bar and into a smaller room near the back of the bar. When the door swished shut, Brenna took a seat at one end of the table and motioned for Lexxa to take the other. The room wasn't anything special, just a small room with a table and a couple chairs where business deals could be hashed out without anyone eavesdropping. Lexxa wasn't fooled, though. She knew that Brenna charged an exorbitant sum for use of the room and then recorded everything going on in it anyway. 'Information brokering' was what Brenna called it.

"So I understand you're in Dutch with FleetCom," Brenna said, leaning back in her chair and casting a knowing eye at Lexxa.

"How could you have possibly learned that in the past ten minutes?"

"You'd be surprised at how fast information ends up going through Conways."

"No, I probably wouldn't," Lexxa admitted and then got right to the point. "I need a crew."

"Well, you're bound to find one in here," Brenna said. "What kind of ship?"

"Top of the line, FleetCom next generation destroyer."

Brenna blew out a whistle of admiration. "You know, for someone who swore off smuggling, you jumped right back in with both feet if you snagged a high value FleetCom target."

"It wasn't by design," Lexxa countered.

"And yet, here you are," Brenna smiled, spreading her hands in acceptance. "Looking for anyone in particular?"

"Just some spacers I can put some trust in."

"Well, you might find some talent in here, but I don't know how well you'll be able to trust them."

"Anyone in particular that you know is trying to get on with a ship?"

"How long do you have?"

"Not long," Lexxa said. "I'm still flying blind here, to be honest. But suffice it to say, I have a warship that I need to keep safe until I can figure out what's going on with the Confederation."

"Give me two hours."

"That enough time to get the dirt on me?" Lexxa asked. "Or are you really going to help me?"

"I'm wounded, Lexxa," Brenna smirked.

"Not as badly as you will be if you cross me."

"Lexxa," Brenna smiled, leaning forward and flashing her a brilliant smile. "I might be a lot of things, but stupid isn't one of them." She pushed back from the table. "Two hours."

"All right."

"Go hit the bar, I'll cover your tab."

"You're being awfully nice to me, Brenna," Lexxa pointed out before the bar owner slipped out of the room.

Brenna stopped and looked hard at her and her next words were probably the most truthful she had been in a long time. "Look, I still feel bad about what happened with the Krayht," she said quietly, an admission that was probably hard for her to verbalize. "I owe you for not coming back here and trashing my place."

Lexxa smiled, feeling somewhat more at ease. "Apology accepted."

"I wasn't apologizing, Lexxa," Brenna shot back, but she followed it with another smile and then was gone, disappearing back into the bustling tavern.

Lexxa shook her head and followed her out. She found an empty seat at the bar and ordered a Rigellian Ale, perhaps the only drink she was fond of. Captain Woolston had been the reason for that and she thought back to happier days, when she actually felt like she was a part of something and not just so much interstellar space dust tossed about by solar wind. Her forehead wrinkled in distaste as she realized those days were gone and likely gone forever. With a sigh, she downed the blue liquid and grimaced as it burned deep into her belly.

"Rough day at the office?" a male voice sounded close to her ear and she turned slowly to pick up the speaker. The glare she gave him should have been enough to back off anyone, no matter how drunk, but the man was unmoved. Whether that was because he was unafraid or just plain stupid, Lexxa didn't know.

"Yeah, I know, you've probably heard all the pickup lines," the man added with an exaggerated wink. "But you're not sitting here at the bar waiting for a rich spacer to come by and sweep you off your feet."

"No, and I wasn't waiting for you, either," she said icily and motioned for the bartender to give her another.

"Matt McDowell," the man said, ignoring the insult and hopping up onto the stool next to her. He held up two fingers to the bartender to indicate he wanted the same. "My crew just calls me Boomer," he added.

"And I'm still not interested," Lexxa said, focusing on her drink and trying desperately to push her anger down. She wasn't in the mood for any nonsense and this guy was just oozing it.

"No need to get huffy," Boomer said, holding up a hand. "You're giving off enough heat to melt platinum."

She turned and glared at him again, hoping her look was unmistakable.

It wasn't.

"Hey, it's a gift," he said with a disarming smile. "I read people pretty well. And I can tell you're in some kind of trouble."

Lexxa couldn't help but laugh. "What part of this are you not getting, Boomer," she added sarcastic emphasis to his name, hoping to drive home her point.

It still didn't.

"Look, all I know is what I feel and hear in my head," he said, tapping his temple to emphasis his words.

"Then hear this," she said, staring daggers into him. Before she could say anything more, her comm buzzed and she took out her communicator, a far safer bet than talking openly. Holding it close to her ear, she heard Jirin's words and felt a cold chill run down her spine.

"We've got company."

Renegades: The Judas War

Chapter 12

Dominant

Mordan System, Free Space

"Full sensor sweep," Captain Rydan ordered as the *Dominant* entered into the system, her FTL drives spooling down. Ahead was the huge asteroid field filled mostly with large rocks, some of them absolutely enormous. The debris field had been known since the Confederation had first mapped out the sector over a hundred years ago, but it had been present for eons longer, likely the planetary remnants of a long dead solar system. Rydan himself knew there was something much more interesting hiding somewhere within the field.

"Sensors are picking up a single energy signature, likely a vessel," Lieutenant Curtis replied.

"Can you give me specifics?"

"Sensors translating now, sir. Rigellian destroyer."

"Any identification on her?"

"No, sir. It isn't broadcasting any transponder signal."

"So she's likely a raider."

"What would a raider be doing out in the middle of an asteroid field like this?" Curtis asked.

"Because one of those asteroids is a lot more than it appears," Rydan answered. "Helm, plot a course toward that big asteroid near the Rigellian. Take us in slow."

"Aye, sir."

"A base?" Curtis guessed.

"A base," Rydan affirmed. "Go to yellow alert and raise shields. Comm, hail the Rigellian vessel. Inform them on all frequencies that we are pursuing a Confederation criminal and have no quarrel with them."

A few moments later, she said, "No response to our hails, sir."

"Should we be worried?" Curtis asked.

"Probably not," Rydan answered. "If it's a raider, it's not looking to tangle with a FleetCom battle cruiser."

"Sir, if I may, what is our purpose here?" Creer spoke up from her comm station.

"If my hunch is correct, we'll find the *Icarus* here," he replied.

"Why would Lexxa come here?" she asked.

"Because she needs a crew," Rydan answered, feeling more and more certain of his decision. "She'll come here to find one."

"So, has she truly gone rogue then?"

"I believe so," he answered. "If she hasn't, she would have already contacted FleetCom. Unfortunately for her, at the moment that hasn't happened. So we must assume the worst."

"Will she fight?"

"Hard to say," Rydan answered. "We don't know the specifics of what went on aboard the *Icarus*. But we have to consider all possibilities."

"And if she does fight?"

"Our orders are to locate and detain the *Icarus* and her crew," Captain Rydan answered evenly. "In the event that we cannot accomplish that, we have been instructed to eliminate them."

"Hasn't there been enough loss of life in all this?" Curtis asked.

"A truer question could not be voiced," Rydan agreed. "However, we have our orders. We will carry them out to the best of our ability and with as little loss of life as possible."

"Understood, sir," the lieutenant said. "But, wouldn't it be easier to just beam down a security team and take her into custody?"

"Assuming she's off the ship, we would run the risk of injuring or killing innocents," the captain answered. "I doubt she would give up easily."

"So, we wait?"

"We wait," Rydan said quietly. Inside, though, he was less certain of his course of action. Maybe they *should* send down a security team to take her into custody. Wouldn't the potential loss of life be acceptable against the greater potential of catastrophe should she return to her ship with a new crew intact? But just as quickly came the thought that were it Captain Fredericks sitting in the command chair, he would have worked hard to avoid any loss of life at all.

As Rydan stared at the screen, he found himself, not for the first time, missing his captain and friend.

"Captain," Jirin reported as Lexxa moved through the crowd, letting the general din of people drown her out to any ears that might be listening. "The *Dominant* is in system and has taken up position near Rockfleet. Her shields are up and weapons are charged."

"So there's no way we can get back to the ship without revealing the location of the *Icarus*," she mused.

"None, Captain." Jirin agreed.

Lexxa chewed her lip as she considered the options. There weren't many. And the only one that presented any opportunity to somehow get her out of this would be to let Jirin in on the one secret card she still had left to play. She knew she could trust him and he likely wouldn't be surprised at what was coming.

"Jirin," she said quietly, looking around to see if anyone was overly interested in her. "We're going to have to flip the script here."

"Meaning what?"

"Meaning I'm going to ask you to take command of the *Icarus* and get out of here."

"And leave you stranded?" Jirin asked, his voice indicating how little he thought of the idea.

"Jirin, I'm in a spacer bar. I'll hardly be stranded," she countered. "But the *Dominant* is waiting for us to reveal ourselves. If you try to beam us out, they'll be all over the *Icarus*, and we don't have the crew to handle an all-out fight with a starship like the *Dominant*."

"Then what do you suggest?"

"Take the *Icarus* to a set of coordinates I will give you. A Sector 6 vessel will be waiting for the *Icarus*."

"Sector 6?" he asked cautiously. "Have you decided to trust them then?"

"Honestly, Jirin, I don't trust anyone right now," she answered. "But what I do know is that at the moment, Kovok is probably the only one that might be mostly on our side."

"Or we're on his," Jirin pointed out, "at least while he needs us."

"Fair point," she agreed. "But it's all we have."

"Agreed, Captain," Jirin finally said after a long pause. "What about you?"

Lexxa looked over her shoulder, spotting the man she wanted to talk to. "I think I'll be able to get some help to get out another way," she said, a thin smile coming to her face. "Just get the *Icarus* to Kovok and we can put this whole mess behind us."

"Affirmative," Jirin said.

"Good. Sending coordinates now," Lexxa said, tapping out the commands on her communicator. "Get moving as soon as you're able. I'll be along shortly."

Lexxa cut the signal and slipped her comm device back on her belt. Looking toward the bar, she saw the man hadn't moved and was busy chatting up a pretty bartender.

"Boomer!" she called out and made her way through the throng toward him.

Renegades: The Judas War

Chapter 13

Conways
Mordan System, Free Space

Lexxa looked at the scruffy human smuggler that had snagged her seat next to Boomer McDowell. One glare from her and the grimy spacer hopped down, muttered several unsavory curses, and then hurried off into the crowd. Lexxa immediately slid back into her seat beside McDowell.

"Change your mind, miss?" he asked, giving her an exaggerated wink and then taking a pull from his bottle of Earth beer.

"That depends on what this is going to cost me?"

"Well that depends on what kind of trouble you're in now, doesn't it?" McDowell smiled.

"Let's just say I need to get out of Conways."

"How'd you get in?"

"Long story," she replied noncommittally. "Can you get me out of here or not?"

McDowell smiled and took a pull from his beer. "Well, that's hard to say," he said. "I know you're in trouble, but I'm not certain how badly. You blew me off just five minutes ago and now you're looking for help, so something changed. What is it?"

Lexxa looked into his eyes, before answering. "I'm with Sector 6," she said evenly, watching him closely. She figured if she was going to get his help, she needed to play her trump cards right off the bat.

McDowell started to chuckle, but then his face went neutral and he studied her. "You're not lying," he said softly, reading the seriousness of her gaze.

"No, I'm not," she answered. "But there's a lot more to it than that."

He continued studying her and then nodded. "Yeah, I reckon there is. This isn't some piddly spacer drama, is it?"

She shook her head.

"So we're looking at getting ourselves in a spot of danger, right?"

She nodded this time.

"Sounds like fun," he said, breaking into a grin. "Sure, we'll help."

"What's the cost going to be, first?"

"Let's work that out later," he said, still smiling. "If you're in with Sector 6, there's more value in making additional contacts here than just getting you out of this rock for a chunk of change."

"Very well," Lexxa nodded. "What kind of ship do you have?"

"Confederation Apollo-class."

"Apollo?" she asked, her brow wrinkling in distaste. "That's a Confederation freighter and an old one at that."

"Madam, you wound me," McDowell said, placing a hand over his heart in mock pain. "The *Dark Stranger* isn't just a freighter."

"Dark..." she began.

"Stranger," McDowell finished confidently.

"So you're running around in an old Confederation freighter called the *Dark Stranger*?"

"That's right," McDowell said and then leaned closer, his smile vanishing. "But remember the old adage—beggars can't be choosers."

Lexxa sighed. "Look, as long as you can get me out of here, I don't care what it is." She looked hard at him. "The question is, can you?"

"I can," he nodded and then looked around and motioned behind Lexxa.

She glanced up as a rugged human sauntered over to them, a tall glass in his hand filled with a muddy colored liquid. He took a drink as he looked Lexxa over with an appreciative eye.

"I'm sorry," McDowell said with a wink. "I didn't get your name."

"Lexxa," she answered shortly, watching the newcomer closely. He was bigger than McDowell, with a dark leather-looking vest thrown over his coveralls. Lexxa lost count of how many tools he had stuffed into every punch and loop on the vest and she had no doubt that the man likely had a weapon or three hidden in plain sight.

"Lexxa," McDowell repeated, nodding toward the man. "This is my first officer and pilot and engineer. Greg Renet. We all just call him Renny."

"Renny," she nodded.

"Pleasure's mine," he drawled in a dialect she wasn't familiar with.

"Earth. Old Australian," he answered her unspoken question. "My family goes back hundreds of years there."

"Besides Renny, I've got two more on board," McDowell added. "Patton and Moordenaarr."

"What do they do?"

"A little bit of everything," McDowell said, standing up from the bar. He tossed a couple of odd-looking coins on the counter beside his now-empty beer bottle. "Patton's human, former FleetCom medical, but he does whatever needs to be done."

"Moordenaarr doesn't sound human," she said, standing as well.

"He's not," Renny smirked, speaking before McDowell could. "He's Nusikan. And a real pain in the ass, at that."

"Nusikan?" she repeated, looking hard at McDowell.

For his part, the smuggler just shrugged his shoulders. "You take on what help you can find," he said. "Moordenaarr might be difficult, but he's good in a fight, one of the best tactical officers I've ever had."

"They usually are," she agreed, before adding, "when they're not slaughtering everything that moves. If you don't mind me asking, how'd you get tangled up with him?"

"Used to have a Krayht."

"What happened to him?"

"Moordenaarr killed him," McDowell answered bluntly.

"Killed him?"

"Well, he's a pirate at heart, I'll give you that," McDowell said with a shrug. "But he'll grow on you."

"I don't plan on staying, so I don't need anyone to grow on me. I just need you to get me out of here."

"And to where?" McDowell asked. "I'm certain you'll need me to get you to your ship and that's likely going to be a bit of a journey. So as I said, he'll grow on you." He chuckled and turned away, heading for the transporter room. Lexxa fell in behind him, with Renny matching her steps.

"Don't count on it," Renny leaned toward her and said with a smile. "Moordenaarr hates women. Considers them weak."

"Don't all Nusikans feel that way?"

"Not like Moordenaarr," Renny answered with a laugh. "But don't worry. I won't let him hurt you."

Lexxa looked at Renny and smirked, but said nothing. She wasn't worried about Moordenaarr. She'd met several Nusikans in the past. They were big and slow and prone to spectacular violence, but they respected someone that could dish it right back to them. And that was something she was good at.

The three of them beamed up together, materializing on a cargo transport pad inside what Lexxa assumed was McDowell's ship. She looked around as she followed the ship's captain out of the bay. Before she slipped through the door, she had seen enough to tell her that McDowell wasn't bragging—this was no ordinary freighter. She saw tech from at least a half a dozen species that she knew of and some tech she had never seen before at all. One conduit even looked like it had Umbral technology implanted in it.

"This ship of yours?" she said, following McDowell down the passage.

"It was part of the Naraq Rebellion, originally," he said. "During the uprising, it was retrofitted with better weapons and shields, and the Rigellians gave it a class-4 cloaking device."

"Impressive."

"Not as impressive as it is today," McDowell went on, stepping into a lift and waiting for Lexxa to join him. Renny stepped in right behind her. "Over the past decade plus, I've added a lot of other modifications to it, too. It's got top-of-the-line FTL engines and forward and aft plasma cannons."

"And the Umbral tech I saw back in the hanger bay?"

"She's got a few surprises, no doubt," he said evasively and then squared his shoulders as the lift slowed to a stop and the doors opened. They stepped out onto the bridge, a small and cramped control room, but very efficiently arranged that Lexxa could see. Unfortunately, she had no time to take any of it in before a massive form rose up before her.

"What is this?" the Nusikan demanded, leaning forward threateningly.

"You must be Moordenaarr," Lexxa said coolly and then before anyone could say anything else, she balled up her fist and cracked him across the jaw as hard as she could. Normally, a human hitting a Nusikan would be foolish and do little in the way of damage. But Lexxa wasn't just human and the force of her blow snapped the Nusikan's head back, causing him to stagger backward a couple of steps.

McDowell glanced at her with a surprised look, before stepping between the two of them. "Not the way I thought that would go," he said, breaking into a grin. Then turning directly to Moordenaarr, he added, "This is Lexxa. She's a passenger."

"We should be making credits," Moordenaarr snarled, slowly rubbing his jaw and staring daggers at the woman. "We should not be ferrying around helpless passengers."

"Trust me, my friend," McDowell said, stepping past him and taking his seat in his command chair. "Lexxa has the "in" with Sector 6 that we've been looking for. It will be well worth our time to get her to her ship."

Moordenaarr leaned toward Lexxa, his small eyes narrowing. "I will not forget that, human," he snarled, looking hard at her.

"I hope not," she said, her demeanor cool and in control. "As long as you understand the dynamic between us, we won't have any problems."

"Dynamic?" the Nusikan mocked. "What are you talking about?"

"It's pretty simple," she said, leaning forward herself and matching his stare. "If you mess with me, I'll kill you."

Behind them, Renny burst into laughter. "I like this one, boss," he chortled. "This will be a fun ride."

"Just don't kill each other," McDowell sighed, but there was humor in it. "I need both of you." Turning to Renet, he added. "Renny, get us clearance from docking and get us out of here."

"On it, boss."

Lexxa turned her gaze to the view screen and watched as it came to life, showing the interior of the asteroid. It was called Rockfleet, a massive hollowed out asteroid that housed Conways and several other, less-friendly establishments. It was well defended, both inside and outside, and the last time Lexxa had been here, she had heard the rumor they were working on a cloaking device that could hide the entire thing. She wasn't sure how close they were to realizing that, but Rockfleet had been around a long time and was big enough to nearly hide a fleet of ships inside. Judging by the number of vessels she saw as the *Dark Stranger* began its turn, she could tell it was nearly full to capacity. There were vessels from small one-man transports to massive freighters, and even several cruisers of various races—human, Rigellian,

Krayht, and more. And outside?

Reality shifted back to her as she remembered what had trapped her here in the first place.

The *Dominant.*

She realized at that moment, she was far from safe.

Chapter 14

Dominant

Mordan System, Free Space

"Captain," Lieutenant Curtis spoke up. "Rockfleet's dock doors are opening. Vessel leaving space dock now."

Captain Rydan watched the ship slide from the hollow asteroid and bank gracefully away from the *Dominant*. "Confederation Apollo-class," he noted. "Identification?"

"*Dark Stranger*," Curtis answered after a few moments.

"Captain Matt McDowell," Rydan filled in the blanks, knowing the ship's history. "He fought in the Naraq uprising. He's been playing the edge of the law now for years."

"You know him?"

"I know of him," Rydan said thoughtfully. "And I know what he does. Scan the ship, please."

"Yes, sir. Scanning now." After several moments, Curtis looked up. "Captain, I am reading nothing at all."

Rydan leaned forward, watching the ship disappear around the far side of the asteroid. "They've got a sensor cloak," he said. "That burns an awful lot of power, just to leave space dock."

"Agreed, sir."

"He's hiding something," Rydan said. "Helm, plot us an intercept course around Rockfleet. Shibby, open hailing frequencies," forgetting himself for a moment and addressing her by her nickname. He was a captain; he would have to make it a point to always act like one.

"Hailing frequencies open, sir," Creer announced.

"*Dark Stranger*, this is Captain Sykian Rydan of the Confederation Battleship, *Dominant*," he said. "You are hereby ordered to power down and prepare to be scanned. Acknowledge."

McDowell listened to the command over the comm. "Sykian Rydan," he said, more to himself than anyone else. "Haven't heard that name in a while."

"He was an officer aboard the *Dominant* recently," Lexxa pointed out, not really wanting to explain further as to why Rydan was now commanding the ship. "He's captain now and probably will be a good one."

"He's always been good at what he does," McDowell said. "Question is, how gung-ho is he about FleetCom?"

"Sorry, I can't answer that one, but I assume he walks the straight and narrow. How do you know him anyway?"

"He's a Krayht. Been around a long time. I ran into him as a spec ops officer before the Naraq Rebellion and then again during the war. He's got a pretty extensive resume."

"What do you want to do, Boss?" Renny asked from his station as he watched the scan readouts on his own board. "We're already in weapon's range and he's running with a fully active loadout."

McDowell watched as the *Dominant* slid into view around the other side of the asteroid, the ship on an obvious intercept course. He whistled appreciatively. "That's a pretty ship," he said. "What can you tell me about her?"

"The *Dominant* is a next gen battlecruiser, built for pacification," Lexxa answered. "She's a recent launch and was part of a routine wargames training exercise that went wrong."

"You got specs?"

"Full array of multi-directional phased pulse cannons and four forward lances. She also has fore and aft polaron cannons," Lexxa answered evenly. "Carries a full load of phasic torpedoes, as well as a plasma torpedo delivery system."

"Pacification?" McDowell said mockingly. "Was she built to put down enemy fleets or entire planets?"

"Who needs the Umbral," Renny put in distastefully. "That kind of ship could easily take out an undefended planet."

McDowell nodded and looked back to Lexxa. "I assume what went wrong in your wargames exercise is why you're here on my bridge, right?"

"Something like that."

"Well, it's a cinch we can't stand toe-to-toe with her," he sighed, leaning back in his command chair. "Can we outrun her?"

"Every one of her systems is a step up on everything else the Confederation has, including her engines," Lexxa answered. "The only way you're going to evade her is to use the surrounding asteroids until you can get clear to engage FTL drive."

"That would give them something else to shoot at," Renny nodded in agreement. "I'd much rather have them blowing holes in a bunch of asteroids instead of punching holes in our ship. Took me four weeks patching us up from the last scrap we were in."

"Agreed," McDowell said. "Strap in everyone. Renny, start moving us toward the biggest concentration of rocks, but don't make it obvious." He keyed a button on his command chair, activating voice-only communications. "Captain Rydan. Long time, no see."

"Captain McDowell," Rydan's voice came back over the comm. "I assume you've activated a sensor cloak because you're hiding something. Or someone. Would I be correct in that assessment?"

"Come on, Rydan, you know what I do," McDowell said easily, but cringing none-the-less. He was a little perturbed that Rydan knew right away he had a passenger. "I should remind you, Captain, that we're outside of Confederation jurisdiction here."

"We have pursued a Confederation criminal here who has stolen Confederation property," Rydan answered. "I know her vessel—said Confederation property—is somewhere in the vicinity, cloaked and hiding. Logically, that would put her inside of Rockfleet."

McDowell muted the feed and asked, shocked, "You stole a FleetCom ship?"

"Something like that," Lexxa said again, but wasn't willing to divulge more.

McDowell shook his head and keyed the comm open again. "Regardless of who or what I have on my ship, Rydan, you're still outside of Confederation space. Back off and I won't report your flagrant violation of FleetCom protocol to your superiors."

Behind him, Renny signaled that they were ready and dropped the *Dark Stranger* under a rapidly spinning asteroid the size of an Umbral Harvester ship.

"The value of this target is such that I have no doubt I would be cleared of any wrong doing," Rydan replied. "If you would kindly return our prisoner to us, we can avoid any unpleasantness."

"You seem rather committed to this, Rydan."

"More than you know, Matt," came the reply and the use of his first name was enough to give McDowell pause. But only for a moment.

"There's an ancient Earth saying, Captain," McDowell said. "Every villain is a hero in his own story."

Silence on the other end.

McDowell didn't wait around to hear if Rydan had a comeback. He cut the comm and turned to Renny. "Activate cloak, full evasive. Let's lose him!"

In space, the *Dark Stranger* shimmered into non-existence.

"Captain, she's activated her cloak!"

"Full scan for any and all spatial anomalies," Rydan ordered. "Tactical, full torpedo spread at last known position, maximum power threshold and proximity detonation."

"Torpedoes away!" came the immediate reply

On screen, the torpedo barrage streaked toward the vessel's last position, before exploding simultaneously in a pattern designed to weaken shields and cause distortions in cloaking devices. Besides the concussion damage done to the big asteroid, there was a momentary flare of shield energy, before it disappeared beneath the asteroid.

"I've got them," tactical reported. "Bearing two six one, mark three."

"Intercept course," Rydan said. "Keep them on your board as long as possible."

"The shield feedback won't last but a few more seconds, Captain."

"Lock weapons and fire at will," he said calmly.

"Captain?"

"Do it."

"Yes, sir."

Rydan watched the screen, looking for any sign of the *Dark Stranger* decloaking as his ship opened up with an impressive array of firepower. He was somewhat surprised at how easy it came to order the destruction of a vessel and its crew to uphold his orders from FleetCom. But he had been told that under no circumstances, was he to allow Lexxa to escape. If that meant the destruction of Matt McDowell's ship, then so be it.

"Holy…." Renny shouted, turning the *Dark Stranger* in a hard roll to avoid the incoming weapon's fire. "You weren't kidding!"

"Lady, what did you steal?" McDowell said, holding on to his seat as the ship banked and rolled so quickly that the artificial gravity had a hard time keeping up.

"Just a ship," Lexxa said, watching the screen. She knew the *Dominant*'s weapon's capabilities, but watching the incoming torpedoes and pulse fire was nothing short of impressive.

"Renny, drop us on the Z-axis," McDowell ordered. "Get us underneath them."

"She doesn't have a blind spot," Lexxa pointed out.

"How about a soft spot?"

Lexxa shook her head and then winced as a torpedo detonated right on top of them. The ship shook violently and smoke and sparks rose from one of the panels.

"That one hurt," Renny said. "Cloak is down to 70% effectiveness."

"Moordenaarr," McDowell barked. "Can you find anything on that ship you can break off?"

The Nusikan snarled, his huge hands running across his targeting board. He didn't wait for his captain's orders, simply dropping the cloak and firing the ship's forward plasma cannon. The plasma beam struck the *Dominant's* port engine, but from the looks of what they could see on screen, the shields swallowed up the weapon's energy and the *Dominant* began quickly banking toward them.

"Drop cloak and divert all power to shields," McDowell shouted. "Moordenaarr, give me a chaff stream, now! We need to intercept those torpedoes, if possible."

"Her weapons are locked!" Renny called out. "Firing! Hold on!"

Phased pulse fire ripped across the *Stranger's* starboard shields, punching through in some places and blackening the ship's hull.

"Rydan!" McDowell yelled into the comm. "You are way over the line here, Captain!"

"I have my orders, Matt," Rydan replied over the comm, his voice calm. "Lexxa must be stopped at all costs. Either turn her over to me or be destroyed. Those are the only options you have."

McDowell cast an almost bitter look at Lexxa, before turning back to Renet. "Get the FTLs online and get us out of here. Now."

"Are you crazy, boss?" Renny snapped, looking at him like he was insane. "We're in the middle of an asteroid field!"

"Activate the phase project."

The look of incredulity on Renny's face grew. "Boss, we've never even tested that. You said yourself that it was too dangerous to mess with!"

"Well, it's that or we turn her over to FleetCom," he said, looking at Lexxa again.

She returned his stare dispassionately. She could tell he would do nothing of the kind. He might be a smuggler and operate less than lawfully, but he wasn't the kind of man that would cut a passenger lose to save his own skin.

She hoped.

"We should just airlock her," Moordenaarr growled from his station.

Rydan's voice came back over the comm. "You have ten seconds to comply, Captain McDowell. Power down weapons and shields and prepared to beam the prisoner over or be destroyed."

McDowell paused for only a moment, then motioned to Renny. "*Dominant*, this is *Dark Stranger*," he said, all business. "Prepare to receive prisoner." Cutting the comm, he powered up the cargo transporter from his command board. "Might as well make it look real," he mumbled.

"Course, sir?" Renny asked, his voice shaky.

McDowell turned to Lexxa. "This is your party. Where are we going?"

Lexxa stepped over to Renny's station and reaching down, she keyed the coordinates into his board.

"Course laid in," Renny said, looking doubtful

"It's now or never, my friend. Punch it."

In space, the *Dark Stranger* shimmered and then vanished into an FTL stream.

Right through a large asteroid.

"Captain!"

Rydan didn't need a report. He had seen it with his own eyes. The *Stranger* had engaged her FTL engines. Inside of an asteroid field. Something that was impossible. "Full scan," he ordered, his eyes never leaving the large asteroid that he could have sworn the ship went right through.

"No sign of them," Antony Curtis reported. "Debris fields are negative. They really did it."

Rydan nodded slowly. He couldn't believe it, but he couldn't deny it, either. Somehow, the ship had escaped. But it would not be for long. "Lieutenant," he ordered. "Plot their last known position and trajectory. Tell me where they're going."

Several moments of silence before the answer came. "Epsilon Majora, sir," he replied. "It's the only system anywhere near their last known trajectory."

"How quickly can we get there?"

"Approximately two hours at maximum speed."

"Very well," Rydan said. "Plot a course for the Epsilon Majora system. But get us there in three hours."

"Captain?"

"They're going there for a reason," Rydan surmised aloud. "Makes sense to let the party gather before we show up. Maybe then, we can get to the bottom of this."

"Yes, sir."

Moments later, the *Dominant* vanished.

Chapter 15

The Dark Stranger
Epsilon Majora System, Free Space

"Boss, we're coming up on the coordinates Lexxa provided," Renny said, looking up from his station. "Long range sensors show a vessel, dead ahead. Time to intercept about seven minutes."

McDowell looked at Lexxa expectantly.

"That will be the *Icarus*," she said confidently. During the journey, she had already informed them that the *Icarus* was a next gen Confederation destroyer, a complement to the *Dominant*. She hadn't shared much else beyond a vague story that her stealing the vessel was the result of a deadly betrayal by her former captain. She had only gotten caught up in a much deeper game that she was still struggling to understand herself.

"We should be at battle stations," Moordenaarr growled angrily. "We don't know that we can trust the woman."

"Oh do shut up," another man snapped. He was seated at the science station across the small bridge from the Nusikan and he merely waved a hand in boredom when Moordenaarr began to rise angrily from his seat. "And sit down before you hurt yourself."

"Enough, you two," McDowell said tiredly. "Patton, what do you have?"

"Not much," Jared Patton said, casting one more look of disdain at Moordenaarr before swinging around in his seat and propping his feet up on a nearby console. Patton was exactly what McDowell had earlier described him as—a valuable crew member capable of excelling at a multitude of different tasks. When he wasn't acting as ship's doctor, he could be found running the science station and even the helm, when Renny didn't feel like piloting the *Stranger* himself. Lexxa had found him quite likeable when he had come to the bridge about an hour earlier and she had listened intently as he told some more fantastic tales about the *Dark Stranger* and her captain, Matt "Boomer" McDowell.

He hadn't shared much about his own past other than to indicate he had once been FleetCom Medical, but had left the service after his ship, the Bataan, had been all but destroyed in a fight with a Rigellian battlecruiser. It wasn't the battle itself that had soured him, but the Bataan's orders to engage a clearly superior battleship instead of waiting for reinforcements. He had never figured out who had issued the orders, but FleetCom had laid the blame squarely on his captain's shoulders and closed the book without an investigation. It had angered Patton enough that he resigned his commission, and after forays on several freighters, ended up on the *Stranger* with McDowell as his captain. He had been here ever since.

"We're still too far to be able to ascertain what she's doing," Patton continued, "but we can be certain she's in system, right where Lexxa said she'd be."

"You should hail them," Lexxa pointed out. "Jirin is likely to be a little on the edgy side after what we've already been through."

"No worries," McDowell agreed. "I'm not about to get into any accidental shooting match. We're still smarting from what the *Dominant* was able to do to us." He keyed the comm open from his command chair. "*Icarus*, this is Captain Matt McDowell of the *Dark Stranger*."

A moment later, Patton punched up Jirin's image on the main screen.

"Captain," Jirin said immediately, noticing Lexxa standing next to the *Stranger*'s command chair. "Are you okay?"

"I'm fine," Lexxa answered, suppressing a smile. It was nice to know that despite everything that had happened and the shadow of guilt that was hanging over her, she still had someone who believed in her.

"That's good to hear," he replied, clearly relieved. "I trust you will fill me in on the details at a later date?"

"Agreed," she said. "But for now, we are inbound to your position. We're some six minutes out. I just wanted to make sure you knew that this ship is friendly." The corner of her mouth curled up in a half-smile. Maybe this wouldn't turn out too badly after all.

"We have you on screen," Jirin said. "However, you are not the only one inbound to our position."

"Say again?" she prompted, her heart falling. Had they been found already?

"We are reading an unknown vessel approaching, heading two four three, mark three," he answered. "They are on an intercept course for our position and will arrive here approximately three minutes after you will."

"Well, it's not the *Dominant*," she mused thoughtfully, understanding that this one was coming from a clearly different direction. Could be it Kovok already? Possible, although she hadn't assumed he would be onsite for some time.

"Orders, Captain?" Jirin prompted.

"Hold steady," she answered. "But maintain yellow alert."

"Affirmative, Captain. Jirin out."

The screen went dark and McDowell looked up at Lexxa. "Two's company, three's a crowd. Any thoughts on who the newcomer might be?"

"My guess is that it's my contact in Sector 6. We are rendezvousing at coordinates he provided."

"That might be well and good, but can you trust him?"

For that, Lexxa had no answer, so she said nothing and her hesitation was not lost on McDowell. They passed the next several minutes in uneasy silence until Renny announced, "Dropping out of FTL. *Icarus* dead ahead."

"On screen," McDowell said.

The screen lit up again with the image of the *Icarus* hanging in space just off their starboard bow. Renny brought the *Dark Stranger* expertly alongside the destroyer, but slightly back.

"Raise our shields and charge weapons," McDowell added.

"Already done," Moordenaarr replied in an edgy tone.

McDowell cast him a withering glance, then turned back to the screen and leaned forward in anticipation. "How much longer before our *friend* arrives?"

"They should arrive in less than two minutes," Patton said from his station. "I've got a full sensor beam going, but I can't make anything out."

"A sensor cloak perhaps?"

"Possibly," Patton said. "It obviously has countermeasures."

"Lexxa?" McDowell prompted, but she shook her head. She had no answers to this riddle. "We've got top of the line sensors," McDowell went on, turning back to Patton. "There's not a sensor mask out there than can stop our beam."

"This one can," the man shrugged, shifting his eyes to the screen. "And we're about to see what it is."

On screen, space rippled only slightly as a ship suddenly appeared directly ahead. Lexxa's eyes widened and she leaned forward herself, trying to come to grips with what she was seeing.

Jirin's voice suddenly came over the comm. "Captain, are you seeing this?"

"I am," she said softly, watching the vessel bank to her port side, giving her a full view of it. The ship was a destroyer, almost an exact replica of the *Icarus*. There were some subtle differences between the two, including the fact that this one was unmarked and painted black. It absolutely looked dangerous.

"Shall I beam you back, Captain?"

"Not yet," she said. "McDowell, can you hail them?"

"No need," Patton spoke up. "They are hailing us."

"Well, let's see who just came to the party," McDowell said.

On the view screen, the image of Kovok appeared. His countenance was grim, perhaps even more so than he usually was.

"Kovok," Lexxa said, biting back her sudden anger. While she had expected him to be here, there was apparently a lot here she hadn't been told about the *Icarus* and whatever project the ship had been a part of.

"Captain," Kovok nodded briefly and then looked at the captain of the *Dark Stranger*.

"McDowell," the ship's captain said, tipping his head in a brief nod. "We're here peacefully, I might point out."

"You have nothing to fear from this vessel," Kovok explained, "but we have little time."

"Why?"

"Because the *Dominant* is inbound and will be here shortly," he answered.

"But how?"

McDowell glanced over at Patton and raised a finger. A moment later, the man shook his head. "Nothing on the sensors."

"That is because the *Dominant* is cloaked," Kovok said.

"With her FTLs running?" McDowell asked skeptically.

"Indeed."

"Regardless, how does Rydan know we're here?" Lexxa asked.

"I do not yet know," Kovok answered. "But we must make our stand here."

"Why?" she asked. "Shouldn't we just flee?"

On screen, Kovok shook his head. "It would not matter," he answered. "It would only be a matter of time before Rydan found you again."

"So we fight?"

"If we must."

"Three against one," Moordenaarr pointed out, grinning almost maniacally. "It would be a glorious battle."

"The odds are not on our side," Kovok replied. "The *Dominant* is…"

"What about your ship?" Lexxa interrupted, feeling the anger begin to rise within her again.

"This is the *Daedalus*," he explained as patiently as he was able. "These two vessels are part of a prototype fleet being designed by elements within FleetCom that are contrary to what the Confederation has been about since its creation."

"They were built for pacification," Lexxa said, gritting her teeth.

"The goals of these individuals are more directed at militarizing FleetCom," he corrected, "although I believe there is much more to their agenda that we are not yet aware of."

"So FleetCom is going rotten," she said. "That much I already know. But why does your ship not bear any registry number?"

"Because this is not a FleetCom vessel," he answered. "It was built from the same designs as the *Icarus*, but in a secret Sector 6 shipyard precisely for this moment."

"Where do you get the funding for that?" she asked incredulously.

"Forty million credits for a toilet seat, I would hazard a guess," McDowell chuckled humorlessly. "But never mind that. Captain, am I right in guessing you're about ready to take on a fully armed Confederation battlecruiser?"

"We are going to attempt to stop a coup attempt," Kovok answered flatly. "And hopefully save the Confederation."

"Not with my ship," McDowell said sourly. "I've already tangled with this *Dominant* of yours and they kicked my tin can down the road a ways without even breaking a sweat."

"Very well, Captain," Kovok agreed. "I agree that this is not your battle. Would you be so kind as to please transport the captain back to her ship?"

McDowell paused for a moment, before Patton ended any further discussion. "Confederation Battlecruiser decloaking port side! She's weapons hot!"

"Evasive!" McDowell shouted.

The screen winked out, switching to the imposing view of the *Dominant* bearing down on them.

"We're being hailed," Patton said after a moment, as Renny sent the *Dark Stranger* diving beneath the *Icarus* and away from a direct confrontation with the cruiser. "They are broadcasting to all ships."

"Put it on," McDowell said, pointing at the screen. "But Renny, be ready to get us out of here on my command."

"Got it, boss."

Before Lexxa could object, the screen switched to an image of the *Dominant's* battle bridge. Captain Rydan was standing before his command chair, his hands behind his back and his face unreadable. "This is Captain Sykian Rydan of the *Dominant*," he said. "You are hereby ordered to stand down and prepare to be boarded. You have sixty seconds to comply."

McDowell started to say something, but Kovok's voice cut him off. "Captain Rydan," he greeted. "You have performed admirably under extremely difficult circumstances."

"Captain Kovok," Rydan said, with a hint of concern. "From what I cannot apparently gather with my sensors, you are in direct violation of nearly a dozen FleetCom directives. You have possession of a FleetCom vessel without registry."

"I am," Kovok said evenly.

"And the *Icarus*?"

"Part of the same power play that put you in the command chair of the *Dominant*," he answered.

McDowell started to say something again, but Lexxa held up her hand. "Let's hear what he has to say," she whispered.

McDowell glared at her for a moment, but nodded and turned to Patton, making a slashing motion across his throat.

"Muted," Patton said a moment later.

"Moordenaarr," he said, "target all weapons on the *Dominant's* starboard engine. If this goes south, I'd like to be able to get out of here without them following us immediately afterward. But don't fire unless I tell you to," he finished with a warning.

"Trust me, they aren't interested in you," Lexxa pointed out. "Rydan's after the *Icarus* and now, I would guess, the *Daedalus*, too."

McDowell nodded and then looked at Moordenaarr again. "You heard me."

"Done," Moordenaarr said, sneering at Lexxa.

On screen, Rydan was speaking. "I have my orders, Captain Kovok. I have been instructed to take possession of the *Icarus* and confine the prisoner to the brig to be brought before FleetCom for a formal court martial."

"Lexxa did nothing to warrant what FleetCom wants to do to her," Kovok said and onboard the *Stranger*, Lexxa breathed a sigh of relief. At least he wasn't going to turn her over to FleetCom.

"That is not for me to decide or to comment on," Rydan said.

"Captain Rydan, consider what your former captain would have done," Kovok said, hoping to spark something within the man. "Captain Fredericks was aware of what was happening. He was the reason the *Dominant* lost all power when Captain Woolston went rogue during the wargames. Your Captain had set that up. You do know the only way for that to happen was by someone with command level access from inside your ship."

"I don't understand," Rydan said, his brow creasing in confusion.

"Captain Fredericks knew what was happening to the Confederation," Kovok went on. "He knew it and agreed to do his part to try and stop it. Taking the *Dominant* out of the fight would give us the opportunity to remove the *Icarus* from the playing field."

"By disabling our ship?"

"So that the *Icarus* could escape," Kovok reaffirmed.

"And he died because of it."

"He died because the people we are trying to stop have been one step ahead of us from the beginning," Kovok explained. "He died because he knew what is beginning to happen in the Confederation can be the end of everything we know. I speak to your sense of reason, Captain. Don't let his death be in vain."

Rydan's jaw clenched as he fought a very real battle within his mind. Captain Rob Fredericks was a good man. If there was even the slightest chance that Kovok was right about him, then shouldn't he be willing to consider it? But the words of Admiral Doyle rang within him again. *Apprehend if possible, destroy if necessary.*

Sykian Rydan had never wanted to be a FleetCom captain, but the mantle had been thrust upon him and he had been given no choice but to accept it. Now he was being asked to throw away his commitment to FleetCom, the one thing he had believed in most of all. He cleared his throat and stood straighter. "I have my orders," he finally said.

"Your orders were given not to help the Confederation, but to hinder it, perhaps even shatter it," Kovok maintained, offering one last lifeline, hoping to avoid the inevitable. "Lexxa has, to this point, prevented that schism from growing into an irreparable fracture."

Rydan seemed to hesitate a moment, before his countenance firmed up again. "Lower your shields and prepare to be boarded," he said. "We will sort this out peacefully, but you must surrender your vessels first and foremost."

"I am sorry, Captain Rydan, but that will not happen," Kovok answered, a tone of finality in his voice.

"So be it," Rydan said and the screen switched back to a view of space.

"Oh damn," McDowell muttered. "Here we go."

134

Renegades: The Judas War

Chapter 16

The Dark Stranger
Epsilon Majora System, Free Space

"Moordenaarr," McDowell said as he watched the *Dominant* bank toward the *Daedalus*. "Prepare to fire."

"Captain, you have to get me back to my ship!" Lexxa said desperately, watching the *Icarus* move in the opposite direction as Jirin began to position the ship into a flanking maneuver. As outmanned as the *Icarus* was, he wasn't going to turn tail and run. He was going to fight.

"Sorry, but there's no way I'm going to drop my shields," McDowell snapped.

"She's firing!" Patton shouted out.

On screen, they watched as the *Dominant* opened up on the *Daedalus* with full pulse cannons and a phasic torpedo barrage. The *Icarus* wasn't spared, either, as cannon-fire lanced out in that direction, too, cutting across the destroyer's shields.

"Fire," McDowell ordered and Moordenaarr wasted no time, firing the ship's weapons at a designated point just behind the starboard nacelle. The plasma cannon bolts flared brightly against the *Dominant's* shields, but the ship pivoted in space with no apparent damage. A phased pulse lanced out from the *Dominant*, scoring a direct hit on the *Stranger's* shields and shaking the vessel hard.

"Aft shield quadrant down to forty-seven percent," Patton said from his station, his voice amazingly calm.

"From one hit?" McDowell asked incredulously.

"They don't play nice," Patton added.

"Bring us about, heading one three one mark two," McDowell said and Renny expertly swung the ship around as ordered.

"FTL drive standing by," Renny said.

McDowell looked at the screen and watched the *Daedalus* and *Icarus* trading fire with the much larger battlecruiser. Both destroyers took direct hits again, but a pulse cannon strike from the *Icarus* broke through the *Dominant's* shields, scoring a blackened burn into the underside of the *Dominant's* forward hull. He looked at Lexxa again, noting that her eyes were glued to the screen and he could almost hear her secretly praying for her friends. He knew what she was experiencing. It was a feeling he had shared before in the past.

Clenching his jaw, he gripped the sides of his chair. "Moordenaarr, lock weapons on the location of that last hit. Give it everything you have."

"Captain?" Patton pointed out. "Are you fully committing to this? We won't get another chance to escape."

"Can't see that we have a choice, Jared," he answered calmly. "I've seen too many people die in battle in the past. I'm not about to watch it happen again and not do anything about it." He looked at his helmsman. "Renny, you have full command of the helm. Keep us away from those pulse lances, but let Moordenaarr do his thing."

"I'll do my best, boss," Renny answered as he put the *Stranger* into a sharp banking maneuver, sending it cutting across the port side of the cruiser. Moordenaarr cursed gleefully as he fired the ship's weapons, sending shot after shot of plasma cannon fire into the damaged underside of the *Dominant's* command structure. They were rewarded with an explosion of slag metal and decompressing gases as a small section of the hull ruptured.

"Score one for the good guys," Renny muttered.

"That will keep things interesting," McDowell said, before being thrown violently to the deck as a pair of return torpedoes struck mid ship.

"Damage to the *Dominant* is moderate," a *Daedalus* bridge crewmember reported as she read out the battle damage to Kovok, "but they still have full weapons capabilities."

"How badly was McDowell's vessel hit on that last attack?" Kovok asked, watching the cruiser reposition itself.

"Multiple hull breaches," the voice came back. "Port shields are gone. She can still maneuver, though."

Kovok watched the screen as the *Dark Stranger* tried to bank away. The *Dominant* turned with it and he could imagine that Rydan was probably seeking to take the ship out of the fight permanently, rather than risk another sneak attack. The attack had been a bold move on the part of McDowell, but he knew they were hopelessly outgunned by the *Dominant*. Unfortunately, they all were.

"Helm, bring us around to two five one mark six," he instructed. "Tactical, I need a full spread, all weapons. Warn them off."

The *Daedalus* quickly shifted in space, coming between the *Dominant* and the *Stranger*, all portside weapons blasting into the battleship. Shields flared all along the *Dominant's* hull, but the damage was inconsequential.

"Brace for impact," Kovok said a moment later, realizing what was going to happen.

The *Dominant* hit the *Daedalus* with a full barrage of its own, but unlike the battlecruiser's shields, the destroyer's shields were not able to handle the massive firepower. The *Dominant's* pulse cannons cut through the *Daedalus'* shielding in several place, opening them up to direct phasic torpedo hits. The ship shook violently as the damage spread and several bridge stations exploded in smoke and sparks.

"Report!" Kovok ordered as he pulled himself back to his feet. A cut across his forehead spilled dark blood down his cheek. Ignoring it, he looked over where he saw his helmsman slumped over the controls, one side of her face blackened and burnt.

Without hesitating, he clambered over to her and eased her out of her chair, taking it himself. The screen still showed the *Dominant* as it swung around for another attack run. He began maneuvering the *Daedalus* into a parallel turn, hoping to keep the battleship's guns from giving him a full spread again. He thought he knew the capabilities of the *Dominant*, but this was surprising even him.

"Captain, we have multiple systems failures," one of his bridge officers coughed out. "FTL engines are down. Shields can't take another hit like that."

"Weapons?"

"At the moment, port and aft pulse cannons only."

"Duly noted," he said, working his wounded ship around so he could bring his active weapons to bear.

"Sir, we aren't going to make it."

"One of us has to," he said evenly. "Perhaps we can give someone the right opening."

"Ronara," Jirin said as he watched the *Dominant* as it pursued their sister ship. The *Daedalus* was firing again, aft cannons only, but the *Dominant's* shields swallowed up the energy. The *Icarus* was in a parallel course slightly ahead of the *Dominant*, while he was programming a desperate gambit that would either see them victorious or see them dead. He wasn't sure yet which would happen. "Bring us to station," he commanded. "Full stop."

"Full stop?" Ronara asked.

"Do it," he said, mentally calculating their chances. They weren't good. But it was the only chance they had. The *Icarus* had suffered major hull damage and several non-critical systems had been shut down to power shields. But though weak, shields were still holding, if at a fraction of their full power, and he still had weapons. More importantly, he had the advantage. At the moment, Captain Rydan was intent on the *Daedalus*, which was damaged far more severely than the *Icarus* and listing to portside fifteen hundred meters ahead and below them.

"Full stop," Ronara said, obeying the command.

The *Icarus* stopped abruptly in space, allowing the *Dominant* to shoot past it as it pursued the wounded *Daedalus*. Jirin didn't look at the screen, instead concentrating on his board. He locked weapons and fired as it passed. The ships four forward pulse lances blasted into the

Dominant, flaring briefly as the battleship's rear shields stopped the attack. But Jirin had anticipated that, and activated a power bypass, pouring the *Icarus'* FTL core energy directly into the blast. The pulse lances were able to handle the monumental power increase for only two point four seconds, but it was enough. The *Dominant's* shields died and the lances blasted into the cruiser, tearing through her engines and ripping deep into her main hull.

Ronara watched the destruction, eyes wide, but expertly sent the *Icarus* banking away to avoid any collateral damage from explosions.

Jirin noted his board. "The *Dominant's* shields are down and engines offline," he reported as much to himself as Ronara. They were the only two on the bridge, the other dozen crew members of the *Icarus* manning stations across the ship, trying to keep them alive in the desperate fight.

"My board shows all our weapons red," Ronara added. "You blew every relay on the ship! Did you mean to do that?"

"It was the only way," he replied, finally looking up to see the carnage on the screen. He regretted the loss of life, but felt it could not have been avoided. Captain Rydan had chosen this course of action. He had just been lucky enough to be able to implement his plan and even luckier that it had worked.

"What now?" Ronara asked.

Jirin straightened and sighed deeply. "Now we wait."

Captain Sykian Rydan slowly pulled himself to his feet, ignoring the sheet of pain that emanated from his leg. He didn't need to look down to know it was broken, likely shattered. The *Dominant's* tactical station had blown out completely, sending a piece of shrapnel the size of a chair crashing into his left leg, just below his knee.

Pushing the pain away, he looked around. The battle bridge was ruined, many of the stations molten slag and smoking. Of his bridge crew, he and Shibby were the only ones still conscious or alive and he didn't know if that would be for much longer. As bad as he felt, Lieutenant Creer looked worse, her face blackened and bloody as she slowly pulled herself back into her chair. He didn't know what had happened, only that the battle was over. Gritting his teeth to tamp down the agony, he slid into his command chair and reactivated his holo grid. Miraculously, it was still functional, but as he glanced over the readouts, he knew that would not last much longer. Weapons and shields were offline and there were critical hull breaches in several parts of the ship. The ship's main command structure itself was almost completely devoid of life and life support for the rest of the ship was on auxiliary.

"Computer," he gasped, his face white with pain. There were several long moments of silence before he heard the answering chirp. At least it was still online. "Tactical sensors," he said. "Distance and disposition of enemy vessels."

"*Icarus*, eight hundred meters. Zero thrust. *Dark Stranger*, one thousand four hundred meters. Zero thrust. *Daedalus*, three thousand six hundred meters. Zero thrust."

Rydan paused and looked at the screen. It was still viable, although there was an obvious flicker in the image. Before him, he could see the *Stranger* and the *Daedalus*. Both hung in space, seemingly dead. He couldn't see the *Icarus*, but he was fairly certain it was the *Icarus* that had delivered the death blow to his ship.

And with that, here he was. Time was up. He had been around for a very long time and had lived through more than his fair share of close calls in his centuries of life. But this time, he had overplayed his hand. He wondered what would happen in the aftermath of this battle. Was Kovok right? Was the Confederation truly at risk? Or was the risk actually posed by Kovok and those like him?

Apprehend if possible, destroy if necessary.

Those words rang deeply within his mind again and he realized that he had only one course of action remaining.

Keying the comm, he issued his last order to his crew. "All hands, abandon ship. Repeat, all hands abandon ship."

"Captain?" Lieutenant Creer said from her station, her voice shaky.

"Get out of here, Shibby," he said softly. "Time's up."

"But…"

"That's an order," he barked. "Take the bridge pod. You won't have time to reach the main decks."

"Yes, sir," she said, before looking up, her blackened face taking on a final air of poise. "Sir, it was an honor."

He didn't reply beyond a simple nod of gratitude. He watched her climb over the wreckage of the helm station and disappear into the escape hatch. A moment later, he heard the pod launch, carrying her to what he hoped was safety.

He waited only a few moments, before finishing what he had started. "Computer, activate self-destruct, captain level override. Voice pattern match, Sykian Rydan."

A moment later, the computer confirmed his order. "Override complete."

"Set self-destruct for 3 minutes, ship-wide countdown," he said, hoping that would give his surviving crew enough time to get to the escape pods and get far enough away that they wouldn't be consumed by the resulting destruction of the *Dominant*. "Self-destruct code nine zero zero two. Destruct. Zero."

"Destruct sequence activated."

One hundred and eighty seconds. That was enough time to make certain he carried out his orders. He ran his fingers across his board, activating the proper commands, pleased that the required system still had power. He just hoped it would be enough. Looking up, he watched the energy light up the screen, engulfing the two ships still within his range of vision.

"Just a little longer," he said softly.

"Jirin," Ronara said, growing concern in her voice as the ship shuddered slightly. "We've got a problem."

Jirin looked over his display, seeing exactly what the issue was. The *Dominant* had snared them in a tractor beam. Worse, it had snared all three vessels. Before he could vocalize the question as to why, he saw the reason and his heart sunk. The *Dominant* had activated her self-destruct. And she was going to take them all with her.

"Escape pods are launching from the *Dominant*," she reported.

"Status report on the other two vessels," he snapped, his hands flying over his board as he began rerouting power to systems he would need if they were to survive this last desperate gambit by Rydan. "Quickly."

"Scattered life signs aboard both vessels. McDowell's ship has catastrophic damage. All they have is life support."

"The *Daedalus*?"

"All engines are down. They're dead in space at the moment."

"That leaves us," Jirin sighed. "Why is it always us?" He went back to work, knowing he had one shot at this. "Ronara, lock on to all life forms in all three ships."

"What about the escape pods?"

"Leave them," he said, not unkindly. He knew the starship's pods were designed to jettison at high enough escape velocity to get them clear of a ship's destruction. But the *Icarus* and the others would be a different story, especially if they were caught in the *Dominant's* tractor beam when it blew. "Get anyone still left on the ships."

"Pad's not going to be big enough," she warned.

"Hold them in the matrix, then," Jirin ordered. "Put them on the pad in batches."

"Ok, but give me a minute," she said. "I need to get them all."

"Quickly."

"I'm on it, Jirin," she snapped back, working frantically.

Nodding, but saying nothing, he continued working with his own bypasses. If he had weapons, he could have probably blasted them out of the tractor beam, but he had fried everything just to finish the fight like he had. Engaging FTLs, though, should be enough to break them free without dragging the *Dominant* along with them. If it didn't tear them in two.

"Transporters locked," Ronara reported.

"How many?"

"Twenty-three."

"On three ships?" he asked, his heart sinking. Even with the *Dominant* ejecting escape pods, there had to be hundreds dead from the battle.

"Yes," she answered softly.

"Well, we've done all we can," he sighed wearily. "Now we find out if it's all going to be worth it." He punched in a final command. "Ronara, engage FTLs."

She looked at him for a moment, eyes wide with fear, before turning back to her station as his plan became clear to her. "I hope you're right about this," she offered. With that, she opened up the powerful engines and closed her eyes.

Sykian Rydan felt the shudder run through the ship and didn't even need to look at his board to know what had happened. On screen, the *Daedalus* and *Dark Stranger* were still there, held in place by the tractor beam as the final seconds counted down in the background. The *Icarus*, though, had disappeared from his target acquisition board. A quick scan of the two enemy vessels had confirmed his thoughts. No life forms remained.

He leaned back in his command chair and closed his eyes, thinking back to simpler times as his fingers went to the small metal band around his wrist, a device he had worn for more than one hundred years now.

Seven.

His youth, centuries before. Before the Umbral came.

Six.

His time in FleetCom, years and years of enjoying life, despite the tragedy of losing his people.

Five.

His new assignment to the Dominant.

Four.

His captain, Rob Fredericks. A good man.

Three.

His only orders, after his captain had been killed.

Two.

Apprehend if possible, destroy if necessary.

One.

Lexxa.

Captain Sykian Rydan disappeared as the *Dominant* destroyed itself.

Chapter 17

Icarus

Tyrus System

Kovok stood rigidly at the viewing window, watching the stream of stars pass by as the *Icarus* continued toward her destination. He was not particularly pleased with the encounter he was about to have, but he knew it was a discussion that needed to happen. He just wasn't certain how much Lexxa needed to know. That was truly the gambit he would have to play now.

As if on cue, the door swished open and Lexxa walked into the briefing room. Her footsteps were hard; it was easily evident that she was angry.

"If I didn't know better, I'd say you set me up," she growled, pulling out a chair and collapsing into it. She was exhausted and her anger was palpable. Kovok knew he would have to tread carefully.

"You were not set up," he countered, not taking his eyes from the field of passing stars. "What happened was beyond our control. Beyond our knowledge."

"You are Sector 6," she scoffed. "What part of this were you unaware of?"

Kovok was silent for several long moments, before he finally turned to face her. He noted her anger and instead of fanning it, he chose to sit facing her and see things as she saw them. Leaning forward, he steepled his fingers and looked deeply into her eyes. He saw the bright intelligence she bore, coupled with the fire of a fierce warrior. He understood why the Cabal had chosen her; why they had done what they did to create her. He only hoped she would trust him enough to stay on the right side of what was beginning to happen. If the others felt like they were losing control of her, they would kill her without hesitation. The Confederation needed her alive. He needed her alive.

"Lexxa," he said, his voice low. "I am sorry for what has transpired. We simply did not know the extent of how far our enemies would go to bring down the Confederation."

"What enemies?" Lexxa asked. "In all of this, I still don't know who we're even fighting."

"I wish I had the answer to that," Kovok admitted. "But honestly, we are not completely certain who is behind this, either."

"Then how do you know there is even an enemy to fight? Might you be seeing shadows where there aren't any?"

"I wish it were that easy," Kovok said, shaking his head. "Unfortunately, we know they exist and we know that there is a very real threat to destabilize the Confederation."

"But why?"

"Why not?" Kovok answered with a question of his own. "The Confederation is relatively young in comparison to empires of other races that we have encountered. And the Confederation has grown to be one of the most powerful entities in the quadrant."

"So people don't like us. What else is new?"

"It is more than that, Lexxa," Kovok went on. "Sector 6 Intelligence has uncovered a pattern of corruption all throughout

FleetCom. Briberies, kidnappings, even assassinations."

She balked at that, thinking quickly back to her reoccurring nightmare where she would become just such an assassin. But before Kovok was aware of her reaction, she mastered her emotions and kept it to herself. "To what end?" she asked quietly.

"I wish I knew what their endgame was beyond the destabilization of what has been built over the centuries," he answered. "But at the moment, I honestly do not know."

"But you know they exist?"

Kovok nodded.

"So you had me get involved with stealing the *Icarus*."

He nodded again. "The *Icarus* was just part of the whole and we ended up being woefully short-sighted in the end," he said. "Our belief has been, and still is, that the building of the *Dominant* and the *Icarus* was for a specific purpose."

"Pacification. I've heard this before."

"But the pacification of what?" Kovok pointed out. "You saw the firepower of the *Dominant* and what it was capable of doing. This was not a ship built to face the Umbral threat or some other new enemy we have not yet seen. This was a ship built to match up against familiar enemies and in the end, annihilate not just ships, but fleets. It was an overreach of power beyond anything we expected, and our belief is that the ships were going to be turned on our own."

"You mean Confederation citizens?"

"Exactly."

"You're joking."

"I never joke," he answered in all seriousness.

"So stealing it…" she trailed off.

"Would delay their plans, at least for the time being," he finished for her. "Sure, they can build another one, but will they? After the destruction of the *Dominant*, I am not so sure they will."

"No, they'll build something bigger," she sighed.

"I am afraid you are probably right. But for the moment, they are regrouping. That gives us a chance to regroup ourselves."

Lexxa stood up and went to the window, looking at the stars herself. She supposed she wasn't surprised at what Kovok told her. Frankly, she had suspected it all herself; Kovok had just confirmed it for her. What concerned her was what Kovok wasn't telling her. She knew there were things he hadn't shared. He had his reasons, she was sure, but that didn't make it any easier to stomach. "So, what would you have me do?" she finally asked, feeling suddenly very tired.

"Unfortunately, you cannot go back to FleetCom," he answered.

"I didn't figure as much. I imagine I'm public enemy number one."

"Most people think you are dead," Kovok said. "I have already leaked details of the battle and a Confederation cruiser is inbound to the scene to pick up survivors. For the moment, the story will hold, but once they begin interviewing survivors of the *Dominant*, it is possible one of them will have seen the *Icarus* escape. When that happens, FleetCom will realize you are alive and come after you with a vengeance."

"So, FleetCom will eventually want me imprisoned and this secret organization you told me about probably wants me dead," she said. "I'm surrounded by enemies and once again without a home and without a ship and crew."

"I would not go that far."

She caught the inflection in his voice and turned to regard him, waiting for him to explain.

"The *Daedalus* is destroyed," he said in answer. "It served its purpose in blunting the looming crisis. Sector 6 will not build another for obvious reasons. We were lucky to have gotten away with it for as long as we did."

"And that means what to me?"

"The *Icarus* is presumed destroyed," he went on. "And that thought will continue for some time before the truth comes out and FleetCom starts searching for you."

"You want me to take the *Icarus*?" she guessed, not bothering to hide her shock. "Again?"

"Indeed," he nodded, rising to his feet. "Take it and run. You have a previous life, Lexxa. You can reintegrate yourself with those you once called friends."

"I have precious few of those," she corrected him. "And a lot of those that I did have are gone or imprisoned."

"Nevertheless, this gives you an opportunity to not only survive, but with a ship like the *Icarus*, you can thrive."

"As an outlaw?"

"Yes," Kovok nodded. "Unfortunately, I do not have the ability to change that. Once FleetCom realizes you are alive, they will lay everything at your feet and stop at nothing to capture you."

"Or kill me."

"Commanding the *Icarus* might make that a little more difficult," he said.

"So you're giving me the ship," she stated, shaking her head in weary disbelief. "I supposed I should be grateful, but somehow I can't find it in myself to thank you."

"I am not looking for gratitude," Kovok said. "This certainly does not make up for what you have lost and I am aware you have lost a great deal."

She stared at him, wondering what else she could say. But silence was all that she could offer.

Kovok gave her a tight-lipped smile. He knew what she was feeling; words were not needed. "May you find the peace you seek, Lexxa." Then without another word, he turned and left the conference room. Lexxa stood silent for a moment, before turning back to the window, wondering if that was even possible.

Chapter 18

Icarus

Tyrus System

"How is he?" Lexxa asked as she stepped into Sick Bay the following day. The room wasn't as spacious as it was on a regular starship, but it was compact and efficient, perfect for an assault destroyer like the *Icarus*.

Jared Patton gave her a solemn look and shook his head. "There's nothing more I can do," he said softly, his eyes ringed with darkness. It was obvious he hadn't slept since the battle.

"How long?"

"Maybe a few more hours without the machines," Patton answered. "And that's only because he's stubborn."

"Is there any hope at all if we could get him to a FleetCom hospital?" she asked, although she had no clue how she would pull off something like that.

"No," Patton said sadly. "As I feared, the cellular damage is too severe. There's nothing they can use to regenerate his body and if you mention cloning to him, he'll probably kill you."

She shook her head and slapped her hand against the door frame, anger at the waste of life flaring up within her again. Kovok was gone, having taken the last remaining FTL shuttle and those few surviving crew members of the *Dominant* and *Daedalus*. She was left with her own meager crew, as well as the survivors of the *Dark Stranger*. Greg 'Renny'

Renet had died at the helm. Like her, Moordenaarr and Patton had survived, more or less singed but relatively unhurt. Captain McDowell, on the other hand, had been critically injured. The final attack from the *Dominant* had blown most bridge systems, which sparked a flash plasma fire. The same fire that had killed Renny outright, had burned McDowell nearly beyond recognition. Patton had put him in a medical coma immediately upon being beamed to the *Icarus*, but he had done so with little hope. Now, sixteen hours later, he was confirming it. Matt McDowell was going to die.

"He asked for you, Lexxa," Patton said, then bowed his head and exited sick bay, leaving her alone with the wounded.

Taking a deep breath, she rounded the corner and walked slowly toward McDowell's bed. He was wrapped completely in burn gauze, which would at least keep the pain down. Only his face was visible and she involuntarily winced at the sight. His hair was gone and except for a small patch from his forehead down to his jaw on the right side, most of his flesh still blackened and charred. But one eye remained bright and blue and McDowell caught the look on her face.

"I don't suppose…I'm all that pretty anymore," he rasped, the shards of his voice all that remained of lungs that had been seared with superheated plasma.

Lexxa stepped up next to the bed and looked down at him. She hadn't known him all that long, but she had come to realize he was a good man, someone she would have been honored to call her friend. And now, he was going to be taken away from her like everyone else. For a moment, she felt despair, but that quickly changed to anger at her own selfishness. Matt McDowell was dying and here she was, worried about herself.

"Don't…sweat it," he said, his one good eye twinkling as he read her perfectly. "I've lost…friends, too." He paused, wheezing in enough air to continue. "It's natural…to feel cheated."

"It's not right, though," she said, hastily wiping a tear from her eye. "McDowell…" she began, but he cut her off.

"Lexxa," he gasped. "Promise me…something."

She nodded, swallowing hard.

"Moordenaarr," he went on. "He's a…royal…pain in the ass."

Lexxa couldn't help but laugh, a rough combination of a chuckle and sob. "Yeah," she sighed. "He is, at that."

"He has…nothing. He needs…he needs you."

"Me?"

"He needs a captain," McDowell gasped, struggling more and more to talk. "Take care of…him. Please."

For as much as Lexxa disliked Moordenaarr, she agreed immediately to McDowell's request. "I promise," she said.

McDowell tried to smile, seeming to sink deeper into the pillow. "You're good…people. It's been an honor…to know you."

This time, the tears came unbidden and she couldn't stop them.

"Don't be…sad," he went on. "I'm okay with this."

"But you're dying," she sobbed, wanting to scream out at the injustice of it all.

"Everyone dies," he said and through a last bit of tremendous strength of will, he reached up, touching her face with a bandaged hand. "But not everyone…truly lives."

"William Wallace," she choked, forcing a sad smile that he would reference the ancient Scottish freedom fighter, an old earth hero she had read much about.

Matt McDowell smiled one last time, his burned face unable to mask the sincerity of it. Then with a final sigh, his eyes closed and he breathed his last.

Lexxa held his hand to her cheek and let the tears flow.

Two days later, Lexxa sat across from Jared Patton, a half empty bottle of old Kentucky bourbon on the table between them. Both their glasses were low, so Patton reached over and poured them each another shot.

"Where will you go?" Lexxa asked, tilting her glass and watching the amber liquid ripple along the sides. For as strong as the liquor was, it wasn't doing anything for her right now beyond increasing her despondency. McDowell's death had hit her hard, even though she had known him only a few short hours. Patton had known him for years.

"I'll probably go to Nowhere," he answered, his words a little slurred. He didn't hold his drink nearly as well as Lexxa did.

"Nowhere?" she questioned, looking up. "You have to go somewhere."

"Nowhere is somewhere."

"Sorry, but you've lost me. Care to explain?"

Patton smiled and swirled his own drink, he eyes taking on a dreamy look. "A number of years ago, Matt founded a small colony on a little asteroid," she said slowly.

"A colony," she repeated.

"Yes."

"On an asteroid."

"Yes."

"Well, I can see why it's called Nowhere," she said sullenly and quickly downed her drink.

"But that's just it," Patton said. "It's somewhere."

"Patton, you're drunk."

"True," the surgeon replied, looking at his own drink before swallowing it in two large gulps. Soberness would be a while coming for him. "But you're missing the point."

"What, of living on an asteroid?"

"Not just any asteroid," Patton answered. "Hollowed out and built with every kind of technology Matt could get his hands on."

"Sounds lovely," she said unconvincingly, pouring the last bit of the bottle into her glass. She didn't offer any more to Patton because quite frankly, she was certain he would be passed out in the next few minutes.

"Oh, but it is," Patton went on. "Fully self-sustaining with farm fields and an artificial sun. There's about three hundred people there and room for more."

"You're kidding me," she said, narrowing her eyes. She was definitely starting to feel the buzz herself now.

"No, not at all. It was Matt's dream to build it and his hope that someday he would be able to return and start a family." At that, Patton trailed off, his eyes glassy. But it wasn't because he was going to pass out. At least not yet. It was because he realized that his friend would never make it back to see his dream fulfilled.

For Lexxa, she could understand completely how Patton felt and she felt the familiar rage boil within her again at the unfairness of it all. At that moment, she realized she hated FleetCom with a passion that would never let go.

"I'm sure it's a wonderful place," she finally said.

"It is," Patton sighed, laying his head down on the table. "Someday, you should…you should…visit…" A moment later, he was snoring softly.

Lexxa looked at the man, feeling like he, at least, had something to look forward to. She hoped Patton would be able to find peace after all the heartache. Perhaps he would settle down himself and realize his friend's dream for him. At least, she thought, Matt's memory would live on.

She knew she wouldn't forget him, either.

Her comm beeped and she hesitated before answering it. "Go ahead," she said, a definite slur in her voice this time.

"Captain," Jirin's voice said slowly. "Moordenaarr is demanding to operate tactical."

"Well, we're not in a fight," she said off-handedly. "Not much damage he can do, right?"

"No," came the hesitating reply. "I suppose not."

"Let him be," she said. "We'll try to get to know him a little better as time goes by."

"And if we can't?"

"We can always airlock him," she replied without meaning it. She would honor her promise to McDowell, no matter how much she might regret it. Moordenaarr was an outcast, a criminal even. How much different was he than she was?

"Not much," she mumbled aloud, tossing back the last of her drink.

"Say again," Jirin spoke up, reminding her that her comm was still open.

"Nothing, Jirin," she said, forcing herself to stand. "Just thinking about..." With a sigh, she cut the comm. She placed her hand gently against Patton's forehead. "Sleep well, Jared," she said. "May you find everything you seek…Nowhere."

160

Epilogue

Admiral Armstrong watched the data stream across the holoboard in front of him. He normally considered himself a patient man, but he had to admit that this one had him more than a little angry. All that planning. All their pieces in place. And now they had lost both ships. Breathing deeply to calm himself, he activated the comm link at his desk and went through the standard identification protocol that would give him access. The screen flickered and came to life as a figure stepped into view.

"Masaru," he said, inclining his head in a slight nod of greeting.

"You have a report?" Masaru asked.

"It is as we suspected. The *Icarus* escaped the battle with the *Dominant*. My sources place Lexxa onboard as captain. I do not know or care who her crew is."

"Excellent," Masaru said. "Then all is as it should be."

"If I may be so bold, the *Dominant* was destroyed," Armstrong pointed out.

"Yes, an unfortunate setback, but certainly not insurmountable," Masaru said, seemingly unaffected by the disaster. "The *Dominant* would have played a role, indeed, but the main thrust of our blueprint is intact and proceeding forward."

"That battleship was the crown jewel of the new fleet," he argued.

"Not the crown jewel, but an important piece, yes," Masaru agreed. "Even still, it is no longer in play and our timeline is unaffected. Sector 6 believes they have destroyed a budding insurgency, when in effect, they have actually fanned the secret flames of the disenchanted. They believe by giving the *Icarus* to Lexxa, they give her the chance to evade our plans. But her memory cap is intact and she will do exactly what she wants for now, until we activate her. When we do, she will have no choice. She will bring the *Icarus* to us and complete her mission, as she was programmed."

"You seem confident."

"And why would I not be?" Masaru questioned haughtily. "We have spent many of your human years implementing this plan to bring down the Confederation. We will not fail."

"No," the man finally agreed thoughtfully. "We will not." He didn't voice his other thoughts, for obvious reasons. Masaru was an alien and like so many other non-humans in the galaxy, he was bent on the destruction of the Confederation. Armstrong, however, had other plans for the Confederation and would see them realized with Masaru's help, before he eliminated the *creature* and all those like him. For the moment, Masaru was useful and Armstrong could play the subservient lieutenant for as long as was required. But in time, when a new Confederation was born, he would be in charge.

"I'm glad you are in agreement," Masaru said, a hint of venom in his comment as if he was warning the man to keep his concern in check. "Contact me at the next required check-in with an update. Base construction is still proceeding as planned?"

"Yes," he answered, knowing that they were even ahead of schedule. Regardless of what Lexxa was up to, that part of the plan was untouched. So, too, was the cloning project. Their pilots would be ready when the time was ready to drop the axe across the neck of the

Confederation as it existed today.

"Excellent," Masaru said. "Proceed as instructed. And Admiral?"

"Yes?"

"Give no thought to the girl," Masaru said. "She is fully in our control."

Armstrong nodded and without another word, keyed off the comm. Then, just because Masaru had instructed him not to, he let his thoughts go to Lexxa. And indeed, why shouldn't he? There was much to consider with that one.

Many light years away, Lexxa sat on the edge of her bunk, rubbing at her temples. Her head ached, the result of a combination of hangover and the lingering remainder of another nightmare. But it wasn't the murder of The Admiral this time that had plagued her dreams. No, this one had been different. Darker. It was an image she couldn't scrub from her mind, hard as she tried. A skeletal figure, seated in a captain's chair aboard an unknown battle bridge. Red flames danced in the eye sockets of a skull as it pointed a bony finger at her, silently accusing her.

But of what?

She shook her head and pulled her hands away from her face, seeing them for what they were.

That was when she saw the blood.

Michael Koogler was born in Dayton, Ohio and resides today in Iowa with his wife and children. He got his start as a writer in the early eighties when he wrote an article for the local newspaper and has been writing one thing or another ever since.

He is an avid reader of all things fiction and putting pen to paper is a joy hard to express. He continues to balance his time between work, family, and spinning stories and yarns about end-times thrillers, horror, fantasy, and science fiction.

You can find his website, including all of his available works, at www.michaelkoogler.net.

Sky Conway is the CEO of Atomic Network, Inc. and AtomicBrain Studios, LLC. He is a seasoned producer, screenwriter, creator, futurist, digital pioneer, business attorney and serial entrepreneur. He was an early pioneer and visionary who predicted the Internet would fundamentally change the paradigm for TV and film distribution.

Sky was mentored by his friend Gene Roddenberry, the creator of Star Trek, and was encouraged by Gene to keep the dream of Star Trek alive. Inspired by Gene's faith, Sky was the first to produce original sci-fi content for the Internet in 1999 (when everyone said it couldn't be done) and coined the term "webisode."

Since then he has produced a number of exciting projects, from creating and producing the hilarious short film "Roddenberry on Patrol", in which he parodies Gene Roddenberry's quest to create Star Trek, to producing the sci-fi feature "Inalienable", written by his producing partner Walter Koenig. He then set out to make entertainment history when he conceived, produced and co-wrote the award winning and world's first independent feature-length Star Trek film, "Star Trek: Of Gods and Men", one of the 50 most historic events involving the franchise according to Vanity Fair. It was a huge success and has been viewed by millions online. With it, Sky fulfilled his personal pledge to keep Roddenberry's dream alive.

Sky then co-created and produced his next big film, Star Trek Renegades, which aired in the fall of 2015. It was followed by Renegades, the Requiem, due out in 2017. Sky also created, co-wrote and produced a new ground breaking comedy sci-fi Series Cozmo's. The pilot will be released on the Atomic Network.

www.ingramcontent.com/pod-product-compliance
Lightning Source LLC
Chambersburg PA
CBHW060800210726
48292CB00013B/1546